HERE'S JUGGINS

HERE'S JUGGINS

SALLY SMITH BRYANT

ILLUSTRATED BY LYNNE C. BEACH

North
Country
Press

Unity, Maine

Here's Juggins
Copyright © 1997 by Sally Smith Bryant

Text and cover design by
Write Angle Communications, Camden, Maine

Library of Congress Cataloging-in-Publication Data
Bryant, Sally Smith.
    Here's Juggins / Sally Smith Bryant ; illustrated by Lynne C. Beach.
        p.   cm.
    Summary: When Juggins's father, a lobster fisherman on the coast
of Maine, is accused of stealing from other fishermen, Juggins tries to
clear his name.
    ISBN 0-945980-62-0
    [1. Lobster fisheries--Fiction. 2. Maine--Fiction.   3. Father's and
daughters--Fiction. 4. Mystery and detective stories.]
I. Beach, Lynne C., ill. II. Title.
PZ7.B8405He   1996
[Fic]--dc21

                                                        96-47308
                                                           CIP
                                                            AC

Printed in the United States of America

10 9 8 7 6 5 4 3 2 1

With love to
Peter, Elizabeth, Jim, and Sara

My sincere thanks to

Phyllis Fernald, *for first introducing me to Juggins.*

Numerous literary friends *for their
encouragement and advice.*

Peter, *for your patience and support.*

THE SURPRISE

A long time ago, in a small fishing village called Seal Harbor, lived a little girl named Juggins. Her real name was Sara Bell Tibbetts, but her father called her Juggins because he said she was as tan and round as a little brown jug.

Juggins's house was the littlest house in the village. It was gray-shingled with white trim. It had two rooms, four windows, and a door. For as long as Juggins could remember, she had called her house "The Barnacle." When she was only six years old, she had painted a wooden sign that said "The Barnacle" and had given it to Father for a birthday present. She felt very proud when he hung it over the door.

Her father, big Tom Tibbetts, was a fisherman, and so was Juggins. Behind the house by the side of the road was a board sign with big red letters that read:

T. Tibbetts
Fresh Lobsters–Live or Boiled

and under it was a gray shingle that read:

S.B. Tibbetts
Cunners for Cats–Nice Fat Snails and
Angleworms for Fishermen

Every day during the summer, Juggins and Father rowed out of the harbor in a big wooden dory to haul their lobster traps. They always wore coveralls and rubber boots, and when it rained, Juggins wore a little sou'wester and a yellow slicker just like Father's.

When they came to one of their buoys, Father would grab it with a long hook and pull the attached rope into the dory until the trap came up over the side. Juggins would check to make sure the buoy and the rope were tied securely, and then she and father opened the trap to see what surprises they had caught.

Sometimes there were only sea urchins and crabs in the trap. But other times there were lobsters of various sizes–big lobsters, medium-sized lobsters, and baby lobsters. When there were a lot of lobsters, Juggins would shout with delight. "Oh, Father! Look how many we caught."

Father would say, "They must like the smell of the fish you put inside for bait."

Juggins would wrinkle her nose and say, "I don't like that smell!"'

Juggins always felt sorry for the baby lobsters. "They are so little. I don't like to have anybody boil them and eat them up!"

So, whenever she helped Father take the lobsters out of the traps, Juggins would stand up in the dory and throw the babies back into the water as far away from the trap as she could. Juggins loved lobster fishing even though it was very hard work. Father said she was the best first mate he had ever had.

On Fridays after breakfast Juggins took lobsters up to Madame Crabtree's big, white cottage on the hill. Madame Crabtree had told her that the next time she came with the lobsters she would find a surprise waiting for her.

For the whole week Juggins had been thinking about that surprise and wondering what it could possibly be. Father had had a twinkle in his eye as if he knew all about it.

"What is the surprise?" Juggins finally asked Father. "Is it a big, fat banana?" Father just smiled and would not say a word.

Now it was Friday morning, and when Juggins woke up she remembered that something good was going to happen

to her that day. She pushed back her patchwork quilt and sat up in bed, rubbing the sleepy seeds from her eyes.

The small, bare room was full of bright sunshine, and as Juggins looked around, she noticed Father's bed in the other corner was empty. He must be getting breakfast, she thought. Juggins could hear something sizzling on the woodstove in the kitchen, and the smell of fried cunners was all through the house. She loved the little fish that smelled ever so good, especially when they were cooking for breakfast.

Juggins peeked over the foot of the bed into the kitchen. She did not see Father, but she did see something else. The pans, which they had put on the floor the night before under the leaks in the roof, had water in them.

Sometimes when it rained the wind blew on one side of the roof, and then the rain came down through the leaks at the foot of Father's bed. And sometimes it blew the other way, and then the rain came down through the leaks at the foot of Juggins's bed.

Father and Juggins had made up a fun game about the leaks and the water dripping through the roof. Whoever had the most water in their pan after a stormy night could choose any cup in the whole house to use for breakfast–even the best blue china on the top shelf of the cupboard. When Juggins won, she always chose the china one. It had little pink rosebuds all around the edge, and she felt like a princess when Father poured her milk into it.

Juggins liked the leaks in the roof, and liked to play this game with Father, especially when she won. She felt sorry when Father had said last spring that they must work very hard at lobster fishing so they could earn enough money to mend the roof before next winter. This morning Juggins thought her pan looked very full!

She jumped out of bed in her little, white cotton nightgown and ran to see. Sure enough, the water was up to the brim of her pan. Then she looked into Father's. It was only half full!

"Oh boy," said Juggins again, as she ran into the kitchen to find Father. But he was not there, so she looked out between the red-and-white-checked curtains of the back window. She could see the road, and the field full of wildflowers and lupine sloping up to the big cottages where the summer people lived. Sometimes Father went up very early to Madame Crabtree's cottage with mackerel for her breakfast, but she saw no one on the hill. Then she looked out between the checked curtains of the front window, and there he was, coming up the path from the float. He had a pail of something in his hand, "Good morning," called Juggins between the curtains. "I beat you."

"Good morning, Juggins. You sure did," said Father with a big smile.

He set down the pail under the window, and Juggins could see it was full of wiggling, live lobsters. "I suppose I shall have to go up to Madame Crabtree's with the lobsters myself this morning," said Father, looking at Juggins in her little white nightgown.

"Oh no," cried Juggins as she scampered into the bedroom and began to dress as fast as she could. She put on her blue shirt and her fisherman's coveralls, and buckled her sandals. Last of all, she tied a strip of pink ribbon around her blond topknot to keep it out of her eyes.

Then she ran into the kitchen and was in such a hurry she almost forgot to wash her face and hands at the little green pump. When she was all ready, she got two blueberry muffins from the cupboard and put one on each plate that Father had set on the table.

Father reached up to the top shelf to get the rosebud cup and handed it to Juggins. She giggled and he laughed.

He took the cunners, all crisp and brown, from the stove and put them on the table. Then they sat down and had a very nice breakfast. Juggins had caught the cunners the night before with her own fishing pole and line so they were very fresh indeed. And the milk tasted so good in the rosebud cup, Father had to fill it three times.

After Juggins and Father had finished their breakfast, they went outside. Father tied the lobsters together with a strong piece of string, because the pail was too heavy for Juggins to carry up the hill to Madame Crabtree's cottage. There were three medium-sized lobsters and one big grandfather lobster. Father put wooden plugs between the claws of grandfather lobster, to keep him from snapping. Sometimes grandfather lobsters had very bad tempers. Juggins could hardly wait for Father to tie the last knot.

As soon as the lobsters were ready, Father gave Juggins the string, and she walked off across the grass toward the road as fast as she could. She wanted to run, but it was never a good plan to run with lobsters, because they bumped against your legs. Juggins had known a great many lobsters, and she was not a bit afraid of them, but they were very snappy, and they did not like dangling from a string.

Juggins crossed the road and waved to Father with her free hand. She walked up the path and through the field of wildflowers and lupine, pausing only for a moment to smell the flowers. She thought about picking a bouquet of daisies for Madame Crabtree because she knew they were her favorite, but she decided she had better pay attention to the lobsters.

Juggins walked along, taking a quick skip every now and then. She was feeling very happy thinking about the surprise and wondering what it could possibly be. All of a sudden she noticed that the plug in one of grandfather lobster's claws had dropped out. It must have caught in one of the bayberry bushes along the path, she thought.

So Juggins turned around and walked back to the path. She put down the lobsters and hunted all around in the bayberry and sweet fern for the plug. She hunted and hunted but could not find it, and so she picked up the lobsters and started off again through the field.

She had to walk more slowly now because she had to hold grandfather lobster's snappy claws away from her legs. It seemed a long way to Madame Crabtree's this morning, and Juggins began to be afraid that she would be too late for the surprise.

At last the big white cottage among the spruce trees came into sight and, within a few minutes, Juggins was knocking at the kitchen door. She knocked and knocked and knocked, but nobody came. Perhaps, thought Juggins, Charlotte the housekeeper was giving Madame Crabtree her breakfast on the front porch. She sometimes did when the sun was bright and the sea was blue.

Juggins put the lobsters on the grass by the doorstep, and tiptoed around to the front of the cottage. It seemed to Juggins to be the biggest house in the world, and it made her want to walk on tiptoes. When she came to the porch, she saw Madame Crabtree sitting at a white wicker table sipping her coffee. She wore a shimmery rose-colored dress and, with her snow-white hair and bright blue eyes, she looked to Juggins just like a queen. On the table beside her coffee was a bowl of big fat bananas. "Good morning, Sara Belle," said Madame Crabtree, smiling down at Juggins. "Are you our lobsterman this morning?"

"Yes, I am," said Juggins, standing at the foot of the steps with her hands in her pockets.

"Have you seen the surprise yet?" asked Madame Crabtree.

"I, I don't know," said Juggins looking out of the corner

of her eye at the bowl of bananas. Juggins liked bananas almost as much as she liked lobster fishing with Father, and she was thinking how good they would taste when, all of a sudden, she heard shrill screams coming from the side of the house.

Around the corner came a little boy Juggins had never seen before. She wondered how such a small person could possibly make such a loud noise. He was running as if something terrible were behind him. And indeed something was!

"Why, Jimmy," cried Madame Crabtree getting up quickly from her chair. "What is the matter?"

"Oh! oh, no!" cried Juggins.

"Granny, Granny, Granny," cried Jimmy, scrambling up the porch steps. "Take it off! Take it off!" he cried and he buried his face in Madame Crabtree's skirt.

What Juggins saw was grandfather lobster, with all the other lobsters trailing behind on the string, holding fast to the seat of Jimmy's shorts. Juggins scrambled up the steps after

Jimmy and took hold of grandfather lobster. She pulled and pulled until off he came with a piece of Jimmy's shorts tight in his claw. "Oh, dear," said Juggins, looking at the shorts with a very scared look on her face.

As soon as Juggins had taken off grandfather lobster, Jimmy stopped screaming. He felt around behind him with his hand and, when he was sure that there was nothing there but a hole, he lifted his head from Madame Crabtree's skirt and looked at Juggins.

As soon as he saw her he began to laugh. She was holding grandfather lobster and scolding him as hard as she could for having torn Jimmy's shorts.

"Hello," said Jimmy to Juggins. "I'm going to stay here all summer with Grandmother. Can we be friends?"

Juggins thought for a moment and then said, "Yes."

Jimmy said, "Good, because I'm the surprise."

Juggins began to smile and said, "You sure are a real one!"

BARNEY'S POCKETS

When Charlotte had come out on the porch and taken away the lobsters, Madame Crabtree gave Juggins and Jimmy each a nice fat banana. "Bananas are my favorite," said Juggins. "Mine, too," said Jimmy as he took a bite out of his. "They are one of my favorites, too," said Madame Crabtree. And, as she got up from the table to go inside the house, she thanked Juggins for delivering the lobsters.

Juggins and Jimmy sat down on the top step of the porch and ate their bananas. They peeled them down very slowly, so that they would last a long time. After a few minutes, Tansy, Madame Crabtree's big yellow cat, came and sat down beside Juggins. He was one of the cats for whom she caught cunners. Juggins broke off a piece of her banana and held it to the tip of Tansy's nose, but Tansy just sniffed and looked the other way. "I guess you like cunners better than bananas," said Juggins. "I will bring you some fish this afternoon."

From the top step, Juggins and Jimmy could look off through the tall spruce trees at the ocean, and see the bank of fog way offshore. Suddenly, Juggins remembered hearing Father talk about the Red Robber, and she wondered if he were hiding somewhere in that fog.

It had been misty in the early morning, and because

Juggins had to deliver lobsters to Madame Crabtree, Father decided they would go out to their lobster traps in the afternoon. And now, as Juggins and Jimmy looked out to the ocean, they could see half a dozen little white sails skimming over the clear, blue water.

"I like boats," said Jimmy. "I've got one." "So have I," said Juggins, "we've got two." "Mine's a toy boat," said Jimmy, "but Granny's going to have a real motorboat. A man is building one for her now. Are yours motorboats?" "No," said Juggins, with a sad sigh, "just a dory and a punt."

Every day Juggins wished that motorboats did not cost so much money and that she and Father could have one like the other fishermen. It was hard work rowing the old dory out to the lobster traps, especially when the sea was rough. Father said that all the Tibbettses were made with strong muscles in their arms to row dories with. But whenever Juggins made a wish on a wishbone, or before blowing out the candles on her birthday cake, she would wish very hard for a motorboat.

"Will you take me out in your dory sometime?" asked Jimmy. "Yes," said Juggins, "you can come this afternoon."

"All right," said Jimmy with a big smile. He jumped up off the step, finished his banana and said, "Where will we go?"

"After lobsters," said Juggins.

"Oh, no," said Jimmy sitting back down on the step again. His smile was gone. Jimmy did not want anything to do with catching more lobsters!

"You could take your toy boat and see if it will really float," said Juggins.

Jimmy thought about this for a moment, then said, "All right, I'll get it," and he ran into the house.

Juggins sat on the step looking out at the sea waiting for Jimmy to return. In a few minutes he came out the door, wearing a new pair of shorts, and carrying his toy boat.

"Oh, it's beautiful!" cried Juggins, clasping her hands. And indeed it was. It was painted white, with a wheel like a real motorboat, and it had a little brass anchor in the middle of a tiny coiled rope on the deck.

There was a sailor dressed in a white suit and cap standing at the wheel. Juggins touched the sailor's cap and suit with her finger to see if they were made of real cloth, and they were. "Does your boat have a name?" asked Juggins. "Yes," said Jimmy, and he pointed to the side of the boat where Juggins saw the words *The Squid* painted in bright blue letters.

"Granny says I can go with you," said Jimmy.

"Good," said Juggins. "Let's start now." And she led the way around the house, down the path, and through the field. Jimmy followed close behind, carrying his toy boat.

They had not gone very far when they saw a man coming up the path toward them. As soon as Juggins looked at him, she knew by his squinty scowly face that he was Buck Carter. He was a fisherman who lived by himself over on Back Cove. Juggins was always a little scared when she met Buck Carter because he looked so unpleasant. He was scowling now, as she came along the path. Juggins and Jimmy stepped aside into the sweet fern to let him pass.

"Hello," said Juggins as he strode by. In Seal Harbor you always said hello to everyone, whether you knew them or not.

But Buck Carter just grunted and did not even look at Juggins and Jimmy. Suddenly he stopped and picked up something at the edge of the path. Juggins saw right away

that it was the little wooden plug that had dropped out of grandfather lobster's claw. "Oh," she said, "it's my plug!" Buck Carter now looked at Juggins. "You Tibbettses mind your own business," he growled, and put the plug in his pocket. "Oh," said Juggins again, her cheeks very pink. Nobody had ever spoken to her like that.

Jimmy had begun to run down the path holding his boat very tight, but Juggins stood still in the sweet fern, too surprised to move. Buck Carter turned and started up the hill. Then he looked back at Juggins, his scowl blacker than ever.

"And you tell your Dad," said Buck Carter, "to keep his hands off my lobster business."

Juggins looked up at him with big round eyes. "My Father has never touched your lobsters," she said in a strong voice, although her heart was thumping very fast.

Suddenly, feeling frightened, she turned and started running down the path. She caught up with Jimmy, and together they ran without looking back, until they came in sight of the road and Juggins's house, The Barnacle. Then, when they stopped to catch their breath, they saw another man coming along the road. This time Juggins was not a bit scared. He was Barney Williams, the old boat builder who lived at the end of the harbor. Next to Father, Barney was Juggins's best friend and, as soon as she saw his stooping shoulders and his old blue corduroy jacket, she began to run faster than ever.

Sometimes Barney carried very nice surprises for little girls in the great wide pockets of that jacket. "Barney," cried Juggins., "Oh, Barney, wait for us!" Old Barney looked up and waved his hand. He stood still in the middle of the road with his pipe in his mouth.

Juggins came racing down the path, her arms spread wide, with Jimmy and the boat at her heels. They came so fast that, just at the end of the path, Juggins tripped over a stone and Jimmy tripped over Juggins. Down they went, boat and all!

"Hello," said Barney, as he picked Juggins out of one bayberry bush, and Jimmy out of another, and the boat out of the sweet fern. "What's all this. A shipwreck?"

When Juggins and Jimmy were right-side up again, and

Jimmy had made sure that there was not even one scratch on his boat, Barney patted one of the big pockets of his corduroy jacket. "I think I feel something in here," said Barney, with a chuckle. "What?" asked Juggins.

Barney held his pocket open and Juggins put her hand down into it. The pocket was so big that Barney could carry his tools in it, but now all that she could feel was a three-foot ruler and a fishline. She began to laugh as she felt something else." Are they from Mrs. Milly Willy?" asked Juggins. Mrs. Milly Willy was Barney Williams's nice, plump, old wife, and she was another of Juggins's special friends.

Barney nodded his head. And when Juggins took her hand out of the pocket, she was holding a cookie that was as big as Barney's hand. It was cut in the shape of a fish, and it was covered with sprinkled sugar. "Now it's your turn," said Juggins to Jimmy. "There are some more in there."

So Jimmy put his hand in the big pocket and felt around. When he took his hand out, he was holding another cookie cut in the shape of a seagull. It was also sprinkled with sugar. When they each had taken a bite and after Juggins had swallowed her mouthful, she exclaimed, "Mrs. Milly Willy sure does make the very best cookies." Old Barney just smiled and patted Juggins on her topknot.

"What's in the other pocket?" asked Juggins, walking around Barney. She could see there was something very bulgy in that pocket. Barney's blue eyes twinkled, but he would not let them look. "When we get to your house we will take it out," he said. Juggins touched the pocket on the outside of the jacket. "Oh, I know!" she said, jumping up and down. "It's somebody for the family," she said in a very excited voice. "What?" said Jimmy.

18

But Juggins would not tell either. "You'll see soon," she said. Then Juggins took hold of one of Old Barney's hands, Jimmy took hold of the other, and together they dragged him as fast as they could along the road to the little gray-shingled house called The Barnacle.

WHERE IS GERALDINE?

The bulgy thing in Barney's pocket was a thick piece of wood. It had a funny face painted on one end of it, with a big wide grin and a sharp little wooden nose. It also had a painted yellow jacket, and a ring of rope through its head instead of hair.

"Oh," cried Juggins, as soon as she had pulled it out of Barney's pocket. "She's beautiful!" And she held it out for Jimmy to see.

Jimmy looked disappointed and said, "But it's only a wooden doll."

"No," said Juggins, "it's a lobster buoy." Juggins had a large family of lobster buoy children that Father and Old Barney had made for her. There was Tiny Tim, Geraldine, Mr. Hoover, Aunt Lizzie, and ever so many others. The lobster buoy children were so much more fun to play with. They were like a real family. They could go swimming with her in the summer and sledding with her in the winter, and they never broke their arms or legs because they didn't have any.

They all had big grins and little sharp noses. And they all wore bright yellow jackets, so that Father and Juggins could see them easily, bobbing up and down, on the ocean waves.

Juggins's children spent nearly all of their time out at sea tied to the lobster traps. She missed them, but she saw them almost every day when she and Father went out to get the lobsters. Sometimes she would let the children take turns coming ashore to play with her.

"It's Geraldine's turn to come home today," Juggins said to Barney. "I shall tie the new buoy to her trap, and I think I will name her 'Little Milly' after Mrs. Milly Willy. Do you think she would mind?" asked Juggins. "Heavens no!" said Barney, laughing. "I think she would be very pleased."

Juggins loved all her lobster buoy family, but Geraldine was most special because she was the first lobster buoy child Father had made for her. And today was her turn to come ashore to play.

"Oh, Barney, thank you," said Juggins. "You're welcome," said Old Barney, smiling at Juggins. And, as he turned to Jimmy, he said, "You'll soon be a fisherman, too." Then he filled his pipe and started off up the road toward the boathouse.

Juggins and Jimmy ran around to the front of The Barnacle, and there was Father, carrying a pair of oars over his shoulders. It was time to go out to the lobster traps. "Father, look what Barney gave me," cried Juggins, holding her new lobster buoy child out in front of her. "Oh," said Father, "what a beauty! Barney must have spent a long time carving it."

"Yes, I know," said Juggins, "and her name is 'Little Milly.' I'm going to bring her out in the boat today and tie her on to Geraldine's trap." Juggins was practically out of breath, she was so excited.

Father laughed and said, "I like her name, and I'm glad you are bringing her with us, but what about poor Geraldine? Won't she be sad to leave her trap?" "No," said Juggins. "Did you forget it is Geraldine's turn to come ashore and play for a few days?"

"Yes, I did forget," said Father. Sometimes it was difficult to keep track of all the comings and goings of Juggins's lobster buoy family!

"Can Jimmy come with us, too?" asked Juggins, suddenly remembering her new friend.

"Sure he can," said Father. So they all walked down the narrow, rocky path to the float. Father carried the oars, Juggins carried "Little Milly," and Jimmy carried his toy boat.

There were two boats tied to the float. The little green punt, with the words *Pea Pod* painted on it was Juggins's. The big white dory with the words *Good Times* painted on it was Father's.

While Father untied the dory and pulled it in to the float, Juggins and Jimmy put Jimmy's boat into the water. *The Squid* floated beautifully. "Let's tie it to the float until we get back," said Juggins. "We can pretend it's waiting for a cargo."

"All right," said Jimmy, although he was not quite sure what a cargo was. He uncoiled the tiny rope that was on the deck of *The Squid* and tied it to an iron ring attached to the edge of the float.

"Look at it ride up and down on the waves," shouted Jimmy with delight. "Just like the *Pea Pod*," cried Juggins.

When Father had the dory all ready, he lifted Juggins and Jimmy into it, putting them side by side on the stern seat. Juggins put the new lobster buoy child between her and Jimmy and, although the seat was not very wide, all three fit perfectly.

Then Father jumped in and pushed the dory away from the float with one of the oars. He stood up in the middle of the boat and began to row out into the harbor with long, smooth strokes.

The sky was clear blue, and the bright rays of sunshine danced on the harbor waves. Juggins liked these days the best, and she called them "sparklers," because they reminded her of the sparklers Father bought for her to light on the 4th of July.

As Juggins looked out beyond the harbor she could see a long dark streak of fog against the sky. She and Jimmy sniffed the salt breeze that was blowing in from the sea. They were very happy.

Father rowed out to the middle of the harbor. As they approached Mad Cap Island, they saw a motorboat coming toward them. A fisherman was standing up in the boat and, as he went by the dory, he put his hands up to his mouth and shouted to Father.

"Hi, Tom," he called. "They saw the Red Robber out there again this morning, but they lost him. He went into the fog."

Father stopped rowing for a moment. "Were the traps touched?" he shouted back. The fisherman was already too far away to answer. He just nodded his head.

"Oh, dear!" said Juggins. She had heard Father and Barney talking only yesterday about the terrible things that were happening out at the lobster traps.

"Who's the Red Robber?" asked Jimmy, sitting up very straight and looking out toward the bank of fog. "I don't like robbers."

"He's a mean robber," said Juggins, "and he steals lobsters right out of the fishermen's traps."

"Why don't they catch him?" asked Jimmy.

"They can't," said Juggins, "because he only comes when there is fog so he can hide in it! And he wears a red scarf up to his ears so nobody can see his face."

"Oh, I hope he hasn't taken our lobsters," Juggins said to Father.

"I wish we could see him," said Jimmy.

Juggins stood up in the dory and looked out to sea at the Red Robber's hiding place. "Perhaps he'll come out of the fog," she said.

"Let's watch now, and whoever sees anything can say 'look out'!" So Juggins and Jimmy sat on the edge of their seat and watched the fog bank, with big round eyes, while Father rowed the dory out past Mad Cap Island into the open ocean.

Suddenly Jimmy shouted, "Look out!" "You haven't seen anything," said Juggins looking all around. But Jimmy had—only it was not the Red Robber. Instead it was an ocean swell and, to Jimmy, who had never been out on the ocean before, it looked as if a mountain were coming right down on him.

25

The other end of the dory began to go up and up, and in a moment he and Juggins were sitting on top of the mountain. Then down they slid into a blue-green valley as another swell came racing towards them.

"I think we'd better go home now," said Jimmy in a very shaky voice.

Juggins laughed and said, "It's fun! Don't be afraid. It's like sliding down a hill in winter." And after they had gone safely over three more of the big swells, Jimmy began to laugh and think it was fun, too.

Every time the dory went up to the top of a swell, Juggins and Jimmy looked off across the sea for the Red Robber. But nothing at all came out of the fog.

Soon they began to see little bright yellow spots floating on the waves. They were Juggins's lobster buoy children bobbing up and down in the sunshine. Father pulled the dory up beside one of them and stopped rowing. Juggins leaned over the side of the dory to see which one it was. "It's Mr. Hoover," she said patting him, "and he needs a new grin."

Father leaned over, too, and pulled Mr. Hoover and his rope out of the ocean. And, suddenly, over the side of the dory came a big lobster trap dripping with seaweed. While Father emptied the wiggling lobsters out of the trap, Juggins stood up in the middle of the dory with her feet wide apart and held the oars.

Juggins was a good little fisherman. She never lost her balance, even when they went over some very big swells. When the trap was empty, and Juggins had thrown the baby lobsters as far away as she could, she put a piece of fish inside the trap for bait. Then Father dropped it and Mr. Hoover back into the water.

"We'll give him a new grin the next time we bring him ashore," said Father. "Good," said Juggins, "he does look a little sad."

"I think Geraldine is next," said Juggins, as she leaned over the side of the dory to look for her favorite child. But the next trap was Tiny Tim's, and the one after that was a green-and-white-striped buoy that belonged to another fisherman. Soon they came to Aunt Lizzie's trap and, as they continued along going over the swells, there was no sign of Geraldine. Juggins began to be very worried.

Maybe she was dragged in the storm last night," said Father. "We'll find her further on."

But although they rowed back and forth and emptied all their traps, there was no sign of Geraldine anywhere on the ocean.

"Oh, dear, " said Juggins, as she looked down at the lobsters in the bottom of the dory, for she did not want Jimmy to see two big tears. "That's a fine catch," said Father cheerfully, looking down at the lobsters. "I guess the Red Robber hasn't touched our traps." And, as he looked at Juggins he added, "If you can sell these lobsters, you can spend the money for something special."

"For a motorboat?" asked Juggins, blinking at the lobsters.

"No," said Father, smiling at Juggins, "but maybe a new zipper jacket."

"Oh, Father," said Juggins, looking up at him, "I do so want a jacket that zips." Juggins's old wool jacket had three holes in it and her arms were too long for the sleeves, because she had grown so fast. Suddenly Juggins caught her breath. The fog had crept in and was close to her face. While they had been hunting for Geraldine, it had come silently toward them.

"Oh, hurry Father," cried Juggins. Like all good fishermen, she had learned to respect and fear the fog. Father had seen it, too, and had picked up the oars and begun to row as hard as he could toward the harbor. The gray curtain of mist was just behind them. Little wisps of it were already flying over their heads.

"The Red Robber!" cried Jimmy, looking over his shoulder. "Perhaps he's chasing us in the fog."

"Yes," said Juggins, as she looked back but, at the moment, she was more afraid of the fog than of the Red Robber.

Juggins and Jimmy sat very close together with the new lobster buoy child still between them. Once when Juggins looked back, she thought she saw the tip of a boat peeking out of the mist but, in a moment, it was gone. Then all of a sudden a boat did come out of the fog, close beside them. There was a flash of red, and both Juggins and Jimmy squealed and hid their faces in their laps. When Juggins peeked up out of the corner of her eye, she could see it was only Old Barney in his motorboat. He had been out checking his traps, too, and he was waving his red handkerchief at them as he went chugging by.

The dory moved on toward the harbor with the long smooth strokes of Father's oars. Soon they were going in past Mad Cap Island, with clear blue water ahead. They had beaten the fog and the Red Robber.

When they slid safely up to the float, and Father had lifted Juggins and Jimmy out of the dory, the first thing they saw was *The Squid*. It had a real cargo on it's deck. Somebody had left a fishing line on a reel, with a hook and sinker.

"It's for you, Jimmy," said Juggins. "Barney left it." "I felt it in his pocket."

"Now I can go fishing, too," said Jimmy, looking very pleased.

"We'll go right after dinner," said Juggins.

Jimmy untied *The Squid* and, with his boat and fishing line in his hands, he scampered up the narrow rocky path. He wanted to have his dinner as soon as he could. Halfway up the path, he looked back at the float and called to Juggins, "I think you're my best friend."

Juggins stood in the middle of the float and smiled and waved at Jimmy, but she was not very happy. She was thinking about Geraldine and wishing she knew what had happened to her. But if Juggins had really known where poor Geraldine was, she would have been very sad indeed.

CUNNERS FOR CATS

As soon as Juggins had finished her dinner, she took an empty coffee can from the shelf and picked up the small garden spade by the kitchen door. Then she went out into the potato patch behind the house to dig for angleworms. It was a very rocky little potato patch, and Juggins liked digging there best because she always found lots of worms hiding under the rocks. When Father went fishing on Fresh Pond once a week, he needed the worms for bait.

She got down on her knees among the plants and began to scoop out a hole in the soft earth. Then she turned over a rock next to the hole and there were two fat brown worms wiggling about. She picked them up, brushed the dirt off them carefully, and dropped them into the empty can. As she continued busily digging away, she thought about Jimmy. He must have finished his dinner long ago, so he should be coming soon.

As she looked up through the potato plants she saw two tall slim legs walking toward her on the dirt road. They were not Jimmy's because they wore long creased trousers and had large beautiful sport shoes at the end of them. Juggins went on digging with her garden spade until the legs stopped right in front of the potato patch. Then she sat back on the heels of her sandals and looked up.

31

She saw at once the legs belonged to the new young man who had come to live in the summer cottage next to Madame Crabtree's. He was reading the words on the shingle sign by the road, and Juggins thought he looked most pleasant. When he had finished reading he turned to Juggins and said, "Are you S.B. Tibbetts?"

"Yes," answered Juggins. "Well, then. What's the price of angleworms today?" he inquired.

"They're one cent for each," replied Juggins. The young man whistled and said, "Are they nice and fat?"

"Oh, yes," said Juggins, and she held up a fat brown one between her finger and thumb for him to see.

"Then I'll take thirty," he said. "Oh!" exclaimed Juggins, thinking this was a very large order, indeed. The coffee can was already half full, so she tipped the worms carefully out of it and began to count. "Shall I put them in your pocket?" she asked, after she had counted out thirty.

"Well–no," said the young man, "I don't think so. They might crawl out, and it so happens that the friend I am going fishing with doesn't care for angleworms–except on a hook. Here, suppose you put them in this." He reached into his pocket and pulled out a tin candy box that he handed to Juggins.

She recognized the box because Mrs. Milly Willy had them in her store filled with the most delicious chocolate mints. Juggins took the candy box and packed the angleworms inside. It was a tight fit, and the worms could not have been at all comfortable, but she managed to get them all in. "I had to put in two thin ones," said Juggins, "but they were extra long."

"That's good," said the young man, and he gave Juggins three shiny dimes. Then he put the tin box in his pocket and started back down the road. He turned at the bend and waved his hand, but Juggins did not see him, for she was looking up in the field at something that was coming down the path through the lupine, the bayberry, and the sweet fern. What she saw was Jimmy's very blond head bobbing along above the tops of the flowers and bushes. Below his head he looked very strange, indeed. And as he ran out from the path into the road, Juggins stood up straight in the potato patch and stared harder than ever. He had changed during the dinner hour and gotten very fat around his middle.

Juggins wondered what he could have possibly eaten to make him look so strange. As Jimmy got closer to her, she realized it wasn't anything he had eaten that made him look so funny. It was what he was wearing!

"What's that you've got on?" asked Juggins, as Jimmy came up to her a little out of breath. She tried hard not to giggle, because she knew it was not polite to laugh at people, but Jimmy did look very funny.

"It's a cork jacket," said Jimmy. "Grandmother says I have to wear it when I play near the water, so I'll float if I fall in. Are we going fishing now?"

"Yes," said Juggins, "we must catch some cunners for Tansy and for Mrs. Milly Willy's cat." Juggins picked up the can of worms and the garden spade. Together she and Jimmy walked around to the front of The Barnacle. There were two fishing poles leaning up against the house beside the door. One of them had a line on it. That was Juggins's. She tied Jimmy's line to the other and handed it to him. Then she put the can of angleworms on the doorstep and picked up the can of snails she always had beside her fishing pole.

"When you go fishing in salt water, you can't use angleworms," she said to Jimmy, as they started down the rocky little path to the float. When they got to the float, Juggins put one of the snails on Jimmy's hook and one on hers. Then she showed him how to throw his line into the water. They stood side by side at the edge of the float, and Jimmy did just what Juggins did.

All at once Jimmy began to jump up and down. "Oh, oh!" he shouted. "Something's got hold of my line and pulling it away! Oh, no," he yelled holding on to his pole with both hands, while jumping about in his cork jacket. As Juggins watched she was sure he would fall into the water.

"You've got a bite!" cried Juggins, as soon as she could stop laughing. She took hold of his pole and jerked it up into the air. There, on Jimmy's hook, was a nice big cunner. Jimmy was very proud and pleased when he saw that he had really caught a fish–his first, ever.

Juggins took the cunner off for him and put another snail on his hook. They continued to fish and very soon Juggins caught a fish and then Jimmy had another bite. This time he did not jump around but he did shout, "Oh, I have another." He was so excited. He jerked his line into the air, just the way Juggins did, and landed his own fish right in the middle of the float.

They fished until they had each caught four cunners and, then, Juggins said that was enough for today. So they lifted their lines out of the water and Juggins secured the hooks. Then they turned to pick up their fish and stared down in amazement at the float. And they stared very hard for there was not a cunner to be seen. Then they heard the flapping of wings overhead.

And Juggins cried, "The gulls!" Sure enough. When they looked up in the air, there was the tail of their last cunner dangling from the beak of a large seagull.

"Oh, no!" cried Jimmy in despair. "Never mind," said Juggins. "We can catch two more. That will be one for each cat." So they threw their lines back into the water again, and soon they each had a bite.

"They're the biggest ones of all," said Juggins, as she took the fish off the hooks. She put her cunner in one of the breast pockets of her overalls, and she put Jimmy's cunner in her other pocket, because his pocket was covered up by the cork jacket. Juggins thought that the cunners looked very large with their heads sticking out.

She and Jimmy left their fishing poles by the doorstep of The Barnacle and started along the road toward Mrs. Milly Willy's. Barney and Mrs. Milly Willy owned the general store at the end of the harbor, and Mrs. Milly Willy worked there every day when Old Barney was building boats.

"After we see Mrs. Milly Willy," said Juggins, "we can go see your grandmother's motorboat at the boatyard. Barney is

35

building it and it's beautiful." Juggins sighed a little as she always did when she thought of motorboats.

The road wound around the edge of the harbor, and as they walked along they passed many fishermen's cottages. Most of them were bigger than Juggins's little gray Barnacle. In the biggest one of all lived Jasper Beach, the constable. "The constable is what they call the policeman in Seal Harbor," Juggins explained to Jimmy.

Every day Jasper Beach sat on his side porch and watched people going by on the road and, once in awhile, he took somebody off to jail. He was sitting on his porch today, in his shirt sleeves, looking very solemn as Juggins and Jimmy went walking by. When he saw Jimmy's cork jacket, and the heads of the cunners sticking out of Juggins's pockets, he leaned forward in his chair and stared at them over his spectacles. Juggins and Jimmy kept walking as fast as their legs could carry them and, when they came to the bend in the road, they began to run, never stopping until they had run up the steps of the general store and were safely inside. Mrs. Milly Willy, plump and looking most cheerful in a pink cotton dress, was sitting behind the counter making a hooked rug.

"Well, Lord love a duck!" said Mrs. Milly, looking at Juggins and Jimmy. "What's all this commotion about?"

"We've got a fish for Muffin," said Juggins. Muffin was Mrs. Milly Willy's gray-and-white cat.

"I see you have," said Mrs. Milly Willy, gazing at Juggins's pockets, "and Muffin has something for you, too."

"What?" asked Jimmy. Just then Muffin herself came around the corner and ran behind the counter. "Is it what you said you'd give me the next time you had any?" asked Juggins.

"It sure is," said Mrs. Milly Willy, looking merrily at Juggins and Jimmy.

"Oh, boy!" said Juggins, and she ran behind the counter to see. What she saw beside Mrs. Milly Willy's feet was a box filled with soft hay and inside, nestled together, were Muffin and two tiny fluffy gray kittens.

"Oh, Mrs. Milly Willy," cried Juggins. "They're beautiful. Which one can I have?"

"Whichever one you want," said Mrs. Milly Willy.

Juggins picked up one of the fluff balls very carefully by the back of it's neck and Jimmy picked up the other. "I'll have this one, with the black nose and the four white paws," said Juggins. "They look like little mittens on her feet!"

"Yes, they do," said Mrs. Milly Willy, smiling at Juggins. "Maybe that would be a good name for your kitten."

"Oh, yes," cried Juggins. "That's a perfect name. Mittens it will be! Oh, thank you, Mrs. Milly Willy. When can I take it home?"

"Well," said Mrs. Milly Willy, "I think if I were you I'd wait until it likes cunners."

Juggins took a cunner out of her pocket and held it to the little black nose. "Oh, dear," she said after a minute. "I guess I'll have to wait a pretty long time."

"Just a few weeks," said Mrs. Milly Willy. "But you can come visit her whenever you like."

So Juggins and Jimmy put the tiny kittens back into the box. Then Juggins gave her cunner to Muffin who liked it right away and ran off with it behind a flour barrel.

JUGGINS SELLS THE LOBSTERS

*T*here were lots of barrels and boxes around Mrs. Milly Willy's store. There were shelves, too, full of cans and packages of things to eat. Some shelves were full of colored cotton cloth and ribbons, and other shelves were stocked with fishermen's gear and gloves. There was also a glass case on the counter with gum drops, jelly beans, licorice, and chocolate mice in it. It seemed to Juggins that there was everything that anybody could possibly want in Mrs. Milly Willy's store. Best of all, there was a rope high up across the front window, and on it hung a row of jackets that zipped.

Juggins ran across the store and looked up at the jackets. Yesterday Mrs. Milly Willy had let her try on a little red-and blue-plaid one that was exactly the right size. Juggins had been afraid ever since that somebody else would take it away before she and Father could sell enough lobsters to buy it. Now she could not see it at all among the red, green, and gray jackets for the big fishermen. Juggins walked back and forth reaching up to try to push the jackets apart. Then all at once she saw it tucked in behind a big gray one.

"There it is!" she cried. "Do you think it will wait for me, Mrs. Milly Willy?"

"Yes, I think it will," said Mrs. Milly Willy cheerfully.

Juggins wished that a person didn't have to wait for quite

so many things. Mrs. Milly Willy now opened the glass case and took out two chocolate mice–one for Juggins and one for Jimmy. Whenever Juggins brought cunners for Muffin, Mrs. Milly Willy always gave her one of the chocolate mice. They were Juggins's favorite. They had pink peppermint eyes and long elastic tails and they were much too beautiful to eat. But, in just a moment, there was nothing left of them but the two elastic tails.

"Now let's go and see the boat," said Juggins to Jimmy. So they said goodbye to Mrs. Milly Willy and the kittens and ran out of the store down the grassy slope toward the harbor. They could see the motorboat gleaming white in an open shed down by the edge of the water.

"Barney's painting it," said Juggins, "and it's almost finished. Perhaps he'll let us help." When they got to the shed, Barney was not there. The boat was standing very big and high, across some blocks of wood just off the floor. When it was all finished, Barney would push it off the blocks, out through the front of the shed, and down a sort of little runway into the water. Barney called this launching the boat.

Juggins loved launchings because you never knew whether boats were really going to float until they slid down into the water. She was always excited and a little afraid that they wouldn't, but Barney's always did.

Juggins ran up to the side of the boat and stood on tiptoes, peeping over the high, curving rim. "It's wonderful," she said, feeling the smooth wood and sniffing the fresh smell of spruce.

"I'll take you out in it when Grandmother gets it," said Jimmy proudly. "Do you think we can catch the Red Robber with this boat?"

"Yes," said Juggins." I can see the place for the engine and it looks very big."

Jimmy tried to peep over the rim, too, but he couldn't because his cork jacket got in the way. So he ran around to the other side, thinking he could get a better look, and nearly tripped over a can of paint.

"There's some paint here," he cried. Juggins ran around to look and, sure enough, there was a can of white paint with two brushes in it.

"Let's finish it for Barney, before he gets back," said Juggins. They each took a brush and began to paint as fast as they could. Juggins started at one end and Jimmy started at the other. It wasn't long before the ends of the boat began to be a beautiful shiny white. So were the tips of their fingers and Jimmy's cork jacket.

"Won't Barney be surprised?" said Juggins. But it was not Barney who was to be surprised first.

Juggins was painting away on the bottom of the boat when, suddenly, she heard footsteps on the gravel drive outside the shed. She put her cheek down on the floor and peeked under the boat. But it was not Barney's old fisherman's boots that she saw.

41

Instead, coming along the gravel drive toward the shed were the very same large, beautiful sport shoes that she had seen through the potato plants while digging for angleworms. And beside them was walking another pair of beautiful sport shoes, only they were much smaller. Juggins knew right away that they must belong to the friend who did not care for angleworms, except on a hook.

Juggins stopped painting and sat as still as a mouse, hidden behind the boat. Jimmy did the same. The two pairs of shoes walked right into the shed. They must have been trying to find Barney, for this is what Juggins and Jimmy heard over the top of the boat:

"He's not here, Cherry."

"Oh, Ted. I don't know where else to go. The lobster roast is tomorrow afternoon, and I just won't have Buck Carter's lobsters again. Who else can sell us fifty?"

"I can!" said Juggins, and her head popped suddenly over the rim of the boat, like a jack-in-the-box. At almost the same moment, Jimmy's head popped up over the other end.

"Oh, " said Miss Cherry, with a surprised squeal.

"Can what?" asked Mr. Ted, rather loudly, looking down at Juggins.

"Sell you fifty lobsters," said Juggins, looking up at Mr. Ted. As soon as she looked up, she saw a funny little white thing bobbing around in the air in front of her. She squinted at it and, then, saw that it was the end of her nose with a blob of white paint on it. Her nose must have hit the boat on the way up. Jimmy looked as if his had hit something, too.

"Are you painting the boat or each other?" inquired Mr. Ted, as he and Miss Cherry tried not to laugh while looking at this sight before their eyes.

"We're surprising Barney," said Juggins and Jimmy almost at the same time.

"So I see," said Mr. Ted with a smile. "Now, about the lobsters."

"Will you ask your father to bring fifty lobsters down on the rocks for the lobster roast tomorrow afternoon?" said Miss Cherry.

"Oh, yes," answered Juggins very quickly.

"And will you and Jimmy come, too, and help us collect the driftwood and seaweed?" asked Mr. Ted.

"Oh, yes," answered Juggins, again with a little jump, and her eyes were very big and bright as she looked over the rim of the boat.

"Good, then that's settled," said Mr. Ted, and he and Miss Cherry walked out of the shed and up the gravel drive toward the hill.

As soon as they were on their way, Juggins put down her paint brush and ran out of the boat shed. She could hardly wait to get home to tell Father about the lobsters. She forgot about the boat and Barney, and Mrs. Milly Willy and the kittens. She almost forgot Jimmy, who ran along the road behind her trying to keep up. When they came to the little path that went up through the field, Jimmy said goodbye. Juggins forgot to give him the cunner for Tansey that was still in her pocket. But since the cunner was white with paint, Tansey probably would not have liked it anyway.

"I've sold the lobsters! I've sold the lobsters!" sang Juggins, as she skipped along the road and around the corner of her little gray house.

Father was sitting on the doorstep, mending a trap, when Juggins came around the corner. "Oh, Father. I sold the lobsters!" she cried with excitement. After she had told him all the news, he gave Juggins a big hug and told her how pleased he was. Then they sat down on the doorstep together thinking about tomorrow.

"Do you s'pose," said Juggins, after a few minutes, looking up out of the corner of her eye, "do you s'pose that fifty lobsters are enough for a zipper jacket?"

"Well–maybe," said Father. That made Juggins very happy, for when Father said "maybe" like that, pleasant things almost always happened. As Juggins sat on the doorstep beside Father and looked out to sea, she thought about what a nice day it had been. It was not until she was all tucked into bed that night under the patchwork quilt, and Father had taken away the oil lamp, that she thought about two things that were not so nice.

She remembered that she did not know what had happened to poor Geraldine, and she remembered what Buck Carter had said to her up in the field, about leaving his lobster business alone. Juggins just hoped that Buck Carter would not be very cross because she had sold Miss Cherry the lobsters for the lobster roast.

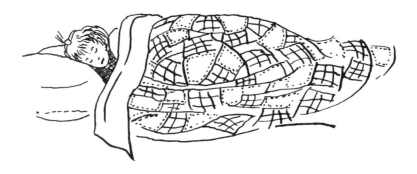

44

And then she thought of the lobster roast and of all the fun things that were going to happen tomorrow. Before she had thought of half of them, Juggins was fast asleep under the patchwork quilt.

THE LOBSTER ROAST

When Juggins woke up on the day of the lobster roast, she did not see how she could possibly wait for the afternoon to come. As soon as she had finished her breakfast, she ran to the kitchen shelf and looked up at the clock

"Father, how many times will the big hand have to go all the way around before we can take the lobsters over to the rocks?" asked Juggins.

"Nine times," said Father, for it was only half past six.

"Oh, dear," said Juggins, staring at the clock. "Doesn't it ever go around faster than that?"

"Not while you're looking at it," said Father.

So Juggins turned her back on the clock, washed the cups and spoons they had used for breakfast, and polished the little wood stove with a blacking brush. Then she looked up at the clock again. "Father," she called, running to the door. "It's going faster!"

"That's what happens if you don't watch it," said Father with a chuckle. He was mending a fish net in front of the house and Juggins wanted to help. She liked to help mend the nets with Father because they pretended that every time she found a hole she had caught a fish. The big holes were whales and the little ones were cunners. This morning the net was an old one and Juggins caught twenty whales. When they had finished repairing it, she ran into the house and looked at the clock again. It had gone around very fast.

"I guess it does not like to be watched," said Juggins, so she did not look at it again for a long time.

She sat beside Father on the doorstep while he spliced a rope, and after that they went out in the dory to get their lobsters. When they got back, they bailed out the boats and had dinner. And then, when Juggins at last looked at the clock, it was after three and time to get ready for the lobster roast.

She put on some clean blue overalls, and scrubbed her face and hands at the little green pump. Then she tied a strip of pink ribbon around her topknot and she was all ready. Father put the lobsters into two big pails for him to carry and one small pail for Juggins to carry. Then they started off along the road to the Point.

The Point was a long stretch of flat rocks at the mouth of the harbor. When the tide was low, as it was this afternoon, it was a beautiful place for a picnic fire.

Before Juggins and Father had come to the end of the road, they could see a column of blue smoke rising above the spruce trees. When Juggins ran ahead and came out on the cliff, she could see a bright fire leaping and crackling between two big rocks down on the Point. Mr. Ted and Miss Cherry were throwing driftwood on the fire. Jimmy was there, too, and as soon as he saw Juggins he waved his hand and came running to meet her.

"I didn't have to wear my cork jacket," said Jimmy, "because there will be so many people here to pull me out of the water if I fall in!"

Juggins was glad because she could not imagine how Jimmy could possibly carry arm loads of driftwood for the fire if he had the cork jacket around his middle. There was simply not enough room for both.

Father and Juggins carried the pails of lobsters over to the fire, and Mr. Ted took some money out of his pocket and handed it to Father. Juggins thought it looked like more money than she had ever seen before. Miss Cherry said that the lobsters looked wonderful and Juggins smiled at Father. She was proud and glad Miss Cherry approved.

When Father left, Mr. Ted said that it was time to get the seaweed for Miss Cherry. So he and Juggins and Jimmy

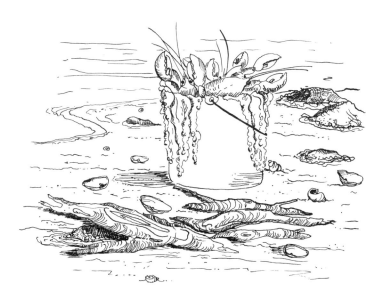

walked down to the edge of the ocean, where the seaweed hung, wet and brown, on the rocks. Mr. Ted had on fishermen's boots today, instead of the beautiful new sport shoes, and he stepped right into the water and pulled off handfuls of the seaweed.

Then he gave the seaweed to Juggins and Jimmy. They ran back and forth carrying it to Miss Cherry. Miss Cherry piled it on an iron shelf over the fire and buried the lobsters in it to cook. Juggins knew just how good the lobsters would taste steamed in seaweed, because sometimes she and Father cooked them this way on the rocks in front of The Barnacle.

Juggins and Jimmy had fun skipping from one flat rock to the next, and jumping over all the little saltwater pools, as they ran back and forth with the seaweed. There was no fog today, just the clear blue ocean as far out as they could see. Juggins wondered where the Red Robber went when there was no fog. Perhaps he was hiding out there among the green islands beyond the bell buoy. She could see the little black bell buoy rising and falling on the water offshore, and she could hear its faint tinkle.

Sometimes when the sea was rough, and the bell buoy was tossed about on the waves, Juggins could even hear it in The Barnacle after she had gone to bed. She liked the sound of it, and she knew that the fishermen out at sea in the dark could hear it, too, and would be able to find their way safely into the harbor.

When Juggins and Jimmy had brought enough seaweed for Miss Cherry, Mr. Ted said that they must have more driftwood for the fire. "It takes a lot of wood for fifty lobsters," said Mr. Ted. "I don't believe anybody can find it as fast as Miss Cherry and I can burn it up."

"We can!" cried Juggins and Jimmy, and away they went. They looked here and there between the rocks, and soon they began to find the pieces of wood that the ocean washes in at high tide. When their arms were full, they ran back to the fire.

Before long more people began to come down the hill from the summer cottages, bringing baskets full of things to eat. Every time Juggins came back with the wood, there were more piles of sandwiches, fruit, and cookies. There was even a sack of peanuts. After a while Madame Crabtree's house-keeper, Charlotte, came carrying a large, red tin box. "It's sug-ared doughnuts," said Jimmy. "Grandmother sent enough for everyone."

Juggins hoped that they would not have to get very much more wood. They had picked up all the pieces near the fire, and now they had walked along the shore as far as Mad Cap Island without finding any more. Suddenly Juggins had an idea. When the tide was high, there was a wide stretch of blue water between the rocks and the island, but now, at low tide, there was a little narrow strip of pebbles on which one could walk across to the island.

"I know," said Juggins. "We can go over to Mad Cap and hunt for wood." There will be lots of it because nobody lives there. So they tiptoed across on the narrow strip of wet peb-bles, trying not to get their feet wet.

The shore of Mad Cap was wild and rough, and the rocks were too steep to catch much driftwood. It was hard climbing, but Juggins and Jimmy scrambled along as well as they could. They went around a bend in the shore, and could no longer see the lobster fire. Soon they came to a pebbly beach and there, at last, were lots of sticks of wood scattered about. Above the beach, tucked in among the spruce trees, was an old tumbledown fisherman's hut. No one lived in it, and its door was swinging loose in the salt breeze, making a creaking sound.

Juggins and Jimmy began to feel very far away from the roast. They each picked up some sticks of wood and began to scramble back along the shore as fast as they could. It was harder than ever to climb over the rocks, now that they had the wood to carry, and Juggins thought that they would never come in sight of the lobster roast again. But when at last they went around the bend, there was the welcoming smoke.

Juggins and Jimmy could see the colorful sweaters of all the people sitting around the fire, and Juggins knew that they had begun to eat the lobsters.

"Let's run," said Juggins, who was as hungry as she could be. But when she and Jimmy looked down at the shore in front of them, there was no place to run to! Instead of the strip of pebbles, there was now a strip of blue water between the lobster roast and Juggins and Jimmy.

"Who put the ocean in there?" cried Jimmy, in a very surprised voice.

"It's the tide," said Juggins. "We stayed too long. It's come in!" And they looked at each other with scared faces.

"When will it go out?" asked Jimmy.

"In the middle of the night," said Juggins, for she knew all about tides.

"I won't like it here in the middle of the night," said Jimmy in a quiet little voice.

"Perhaps they'll see us before that and come get us," said Juggins.

"I hope so," said Jimmy.

"Let's see if we can get someone's attention," said Juggins. So they both stood up on a high rock and waved their arms and shouted as loud as they could. But they were too far away for anyone to hear, and the people at the lobster roast were all too busy eating to stop and look at Mad Cap Island. Far away down the shore Juggins and Jimmy could see them pulling lobsters out of the seaweed and passing the baskets of goodies around. Charlotte's red tin box gleamed in the sunshine, and Juggins thought about the delicious doughnuts inside. "Soon all the doughnuts will be gone," said Juggins.

"They had extra sugar on them," said Jimmy, blinking a little.

"Oh, dear," said Juggins. "What shall we do?"

Just then there was a shout. Mr. Ted had looked over at Mad Cap and had seen Juggins and Jimmy jumping up and down, waving frantically. And now, he was leaping across the rocks in his fisherman's boots so fast that Juggins was sure he would slip and fall.

"You little rascals!" said Mr. Ted, as he walked right into the water. "We thought you had both run home for your suppers." The water was not very deep, and in no time Mr. Ted had carried Juggins and Jimmy safely over to the mainland. Then they all ran back across the rocks, and Miss Cherry and the others stood up and cheered and waved their paper napkins.

There were plenty of good things left to eat after all. Juggins and Jimmy sat on a rock beside Miss Cherry, with paper napkins tucked under their chins, and had all the lobster, sandwiches, fruit and cookies that two little people could possibly eat.

Who is the Red Robber?

While Juggins and Jimmy were eating their sugared doughnuts, they climbed to the top of the cliff at the back of the flat rocks.

"We can see all the green islands from here," said Juggins, "and perhaps we'll see the Red Robber hiding somewhere." They stood under the spruce trees at the edge of the cliff and looked out to sea. They looked up and down the shore of every one of the islands, but they saw nothing moving.

"I wonder where he is," said Jimmy.

"I wonder, too," said Juggins. "Let's look harder." And, as they were looking very hard something suddenly moved quite close to them. Juggins looked down and saw two other big bright eyes looking out to sea. There, not too far from them, sitting on the cliff and looking very small in front of the big ocean was Tansey, with his yellow tail curled around his toes.

"Oh, it's Tansey!" cried Jimmy. "Grandmother never lets him go so far away from home."

"We'll take him back," said Juggins. "Come kitty, kitty, kitty," they said together while slapping their knees. But Tansey was not about to be taken anywhere. And if he could have talked, he would have told Juggins and Jimmy that he came nearly every day by himself through the woods, just to sit in this spot on the cliff. Though he never looked for the Red Robber, and didn't even know there was such a thing, he liked to watch the seagulls soaring in the sky and diving now and again for fish.

Just as Juggins put out her hand to pick him up, Tansey took his tail from around his toes and slipped right out from under her hand. Then he ran off along the narrow path at the edge of the cliff, his tail twitching in the air. Juggins started running after Tansey, and Jimmy ran after Juggins, and when they ran a little faster, Tansey ran a little faster, too. Never once could Juggins get her fingers on more than just the tip of his fluffy tail. They continued this merry chase until the path took them around the turn of the cliff into Back Cove.

Then, just ahead of them, on some flat rocks, they saw a cluster of freshly painted lobster buoys standing in the sun to dry. They had no faces or yellow jackets; they were just plain lobster buoys with green stripes around them.

Tansey went frisking by the lobster buoys and darted into the woods, but Juggins stopped short. There was a fisherman's house close by, and the path led right in front of it.

"It's Buck Carter's house," whispered Juggins to Jimmy, as she peeked around a big rock that jutted out into the path. "I think we'd better go back." But before they had time to turn and run away, the door of the house opened, and out came Buck Carter himself with another fisherman.

"Oh, no!" cried Juggins, right out loud–for there in Buck Carter's hand, swinging by her rope hair, was guess who? Yes! Geraldine! Luckily, Buck Carter was so busy talking that he did not hear Juggins at all.

"Look here," said Buck Carter to the other fisherman. "If they really want to find out who's robbing the lobster traps,

I'll tell 'em. Do you see this here lobster buoy?" Juggins and Jimmy, who were flattened against the other side of the rock, knew that Buck must be holding up Geraldine. "Well," went on Buck Carter, "I picked this up floating around out there in the fog the other morning after the traps had been robbed. And it's Tom Tibbetts's lobster buoy. I tell you he's the robber."

"Tom still goes out in a dory, doesn't he?" asked the fisherman.

"Sure," said Buck Carter, "and so does the man who robs the traps. Is there anyone else around here who hasn't got a motorboat?" Buck's voice began to sound further away now, as the men were walking along the path into the woods where Tansey had gone. In a few moments, Juggins and Jimmy could not hear them anymore. Then Juggins stood up straight in the middle of the path and was no longer hidden by the big rock. Her cheeks were red and her little hands were clenched tight.

"He's a wicked, bad man," she said, with a sob, looking at the woods where the fishermen had disappeared.

"I don't believe your Father's the Red Robber," said Jimmy, trying to make Juggins feel better. Juggins stared at Jimmy and said, "Of course my Father isn't!"

All of a sudden Juggins began to feel very bad and wicked herself. She walked right across the path to the flat rocks where Buck

Carter's freshly painted lobster buoys were drying in the sun. And with the toe of her sandal she kicked them, one by one off the edge of the cliff, down to the jagged rocks below. She watched each one fall as a big tear fell on her little tanned cheek.

Jimmy watched with a scared look on his face. "Let's go back to the lobster roast now," he said, anxiously. Far down the shore they could hear the happy sounds of people singing.

"No," said Juggins. All at once she just wanted to see Father. So she ran into the woods without even waiting to see if Jimmy was following her. She ran without looking where she was going, stumbling over the roots of trees and stumps in her hurry to get back to her little gray house, The Barnacle.

So they thought Father was the Red Robber, said Juggins over and over to herself as she ran along–her Father–because they didn't have a motorboat, and because Geraldine had been found floating.

What would Father say when he heard it? But no, she wouldn't ever tell him the dreadful thing that Buck Carter had said about him. And Jimmy mustn't tell, either. Juggins looked behind her for Jimmy, but he was not there. He must have gone back to the lobster roast, she thought.

When Juggins came out on the road, she stopped running and wiped her eyes on the sleeve of her shirt. She did not like to have anyone see her cry–even Father.

A lamp was already shining in the window of The Barnacle and, when Juggins opened the door, there was Father sitting at the kitchen table finishing his bread and tea, just as if nothing had happened at all. Seeing Father, and being in her cozy, warm house made Juggins feel a little better.

"Hello, Juggins," said Father. "Does anyone want to row me across the harbor to get some bait?"

"Oh, yes," said Juggins, with a faint little smile. She liked to row Father across the harbor and when she did, she would pretend that he was a young man from the city who did not know anything about boats. And Juggins had to help him into the *Pea Pod*, and tell him where to sit, and push the boat off, all by herself.

"Well, then, " said Father, with an extra twinkle in his eye, "go and get your jacket. It's nearly dark."

So Juggins ran into the bedroom and reached up to the hook in the corner behind the door where she hung her little old jacket. It wasn't there, but she felt something else on the hook, and when she took it down, guess what she was holding? It was the red-and-blue-plaid zipper jacket from Miss Milly Willy's store!"

"Is it really for me?" cried Juggins, and a big smile spread across her face from ear to ear. Father nodded his head, and Juggins was so happy that she couldn't think of anything to say.

When she put it on and had zipped it up to the top, she said, "Thank you so much, Father." And together, hand in hand, they walked down to the float and got into the *Pea Pod*. Juggins told Father to be sure to sit right in the middle of the boat, and not to drag his hands in the water. Then she put her oars in the oarlocks and rowed away across the harbor. The water looked all pink and yellow from the reflection of the sunset, and Father was being a very funny young man from the city, so they had a nice row together. By the time they returned home with the bait, Juggins was feeling quite happy again.

That night as she sat on the edge of her bed taking off her sandals, it began to seem to Juggins like a bad dream that Buck Carter had said that dreadful thing about Father. As she put on her little white nightgown, she suddenly had an idea. If she and Jimmy could only find the real Red Robber, then Buck Carter would know it was not Father. They must begin tomorrow to hunt hard for the Red Robber, she thought.

Then Juggins put the new red-and-blue-plaid jacket on the chair beside her bed, where she could feel it if she woke up in the night–which she never did–and then she hopped into bed.

THE SURPRISE ON MAD CAP

*T*he next morning when Juggins peeked out between the red-and-white-checked curtains at the kitchen window, she saw that it was a misty day in the harbor. She could just barely see the outline of Mad Cap Island through the thick fog. Father had said the fog was too thick for them to go out to the lobster traps and that made Juggins unhappy, because she thought it would be a wonderful day to hunt for the Red Robber.

When their breakfast was finished, Father went out in front of The Barnacle to make a new lobster trap. Juggins liked to hold the nails and measure the slats for him, but this morning she put on her new zipper jacket and went to find Jimmy instead. She couldn't wait to show him the jacket, and she must be sure that he did not tell anyone about the dreadful thing Buck Carter had said about Father.

When she was halfway up the path through the field, she saw Jimmy coming down toward her. He had on his cork jacket again, and he seemed to be in a hurry.

"Look!" called Juggins, as Jimmy came rushing up to meet her. She stood still in the middle of the path, and zipped the zipper up and down looking very pleased. But Jimmy's mind was on something else, and he hardly looked at her new jacket.

"Hi," he said. "Grandmother doesn't think your father is the Red Robber, and Mr. Ted and Miss Cherry don't, either."

"Do they all know about it?" asked Juggins, her eyes round with dismay.

"Oh, yes," said Jimmy. "I guess every one knows about it now."

"Oh, no!" said Juggins, with a long breath. "Then we must find the Red Robber right away. And she turned and ran down the path as fast as she could, forgetting about the zipper jacket.

"Grandmother is going to do something," said Jimmy, panting as he ran along behind her. "She says she's going to give a lot of money to anyone who finds the Red Robber."

Juggins hardly heard what Jimmy was saying, because she was thinking about what she could do to find the Red Robber.

"I know," she said when they came to The Barnacle. "We can row down the harbor in the *Pea Pod* and wait at the edge of the fog. Sometimes it goes out very quickly, and if we're right there, maybe we'll see him before he can hide."

As they ran down to the float and began to untie the *Pea Pod*, father looked up from the lobster trap he was making and called down to Juggins, "Where are you going?"

"We're—we're going rowing," answered Juggins.

Father looked out to sea, where the wind had driven the fog to the mouth of the harbor and then he looked up at the sky. He could always tell about the weather by the wind and the sky.

"All right," he said, "but be sure you don't row beyond the end of Mad Cap."

Juggins and Jimmy got into the *Pea Pod* and pushed off from the float. Then Juggins put in the oars and began to row down the harbor. The *Pea Pod* was a wide little boat and quite flat, so it could not possibly turn over. But unless you rowed very well, it was hard to keep it from going around in a circle. Juggins was a good strong rower, and the *Pea Pod* moved along very smoothly toward Mad Cap. There was not as much fog now, and the island could be seen clearly. Jimmy sat in the stern of the *Pea Pod* and watched Juggins dip the oars up and down. It looked very easy.

"I think I could do that," said Jimmy. "Will you let me try?"

"All right," said Juggins. "You can row one oar and I'll row the other." Jimmy moved over on the seat and sat next to Juggins.

"I'll count," she said," and whenever I say a number, you must put your oar in the water."

"One," said Juggins–and splash came a shower of water all over the boat!

"Two," said Juggins–and around went the *Pea Pod* in a circle.

"Three," said Juggins–and up went Jimmy's oar into the air. Jimmy had caught a crab. Not the kind of crab you make sandwiches with, but the kind that makes you catch your oar in the water and go over backwards into the bottom of the boat, with your legs waving around. Jimmy's legs were waving very fast because he couldn't get up with his cork jacket on.

"Someone hit me," yelled Jimmy, in a very surprised voice.

Juggins began to laugh, and finally she put down her oar and pulled at the cork jacket.

Up came Jimmy looking very relieved.

"You can row now," he said, as he sat down in the stern seat again, holding the sides of the *Pea Pod* with both hands.

Juggins rowed along smoothly until they came to Mad Cap Island. Father had said they must not row any farther than this. But the fog had drifted to the other end of Mad Cap, and how could they look for the Red Robber in here, thought Juggins.

"We'll land on Mad Cap," she said. "There's a beach right here, and then we can walk to the end of the island where the fog is."

Juggins rowed the *Pea Pod* up on the pebbly beach, and they both jumped out. They tied the boat by its rope to a big rock, and then they started walking along the shore. There were not so many big rocks on this side of the island as there were on the other side, where they had been the day before. Here they found only pebbles and small stones that did not have to be climbed. Juggins stopped and picked up some empty sea urchin shells.

"When Father and I have ice cream," said Juggins, "sometimes we put it in the sea urchin cups and pretend we're having a party." She put the shells into the pockets of her new zipper jacket, and they walked on until they came to the big rocks at the other end of the island. There they climbed up to the top of the rocks and sat down. Just in front of them was the pounding surf, the open sea, and the fog. It was all very exciting, thought Jimmy. But they did not see the Red Robber.

"That rock's moving," said Jimmy suddenly, pointing to the shore below. "Something's going into the water." Juggins looked.

"The seals!" she cried, jumping up. "They're the first this year, and they always come to Mad Cap. One–two–three–four–five–oh, they're sliding off into the water. Shh. We mustn't talk."

Juggins put her hand over her mouth, but it was too late. At the sound of their voices, the five gray seals, just the color of the rocks, slid quickly off the seaweed into the water. All that Juggins and Jimmy could see of them were five little round heads bobbing up and down on top of the waves.

"Oh, dear," said Juggins, watching them swim away, "I know they won't come back."

"Wait. There's another rock moving down there," said Jimmy. Juggins looked down and saw something trying to wiggle through a crack between two big rocks. Very quietly, without saying a word, they crept down over the rocks to see what it was. There, on the seaweed, was a very little seal with it's flipper caught in the crack of the rocks. It was flopping about, trying to get free.

As soon as it saw Juggins and Jimmy, it's big soft eyes grew wild with fright, and it flopped so hard that it almost tore off its little flipper.

"Oh, you poor little seal!" said Juggins softly, and she knelt down on the seaweed and put her arm around the slippery body. Then she twisted the flipper out from between the rocks as gently as she could.

"I'm going to take it home to show Father," said Juggins, standing up with the wiggling seal clasped tightly in her arms. "I guess I can hold the top of it, but you'll have to hold the tail." Jimmy took hold of the little seal's tail, and they started back over the rocks.

"It's slippery," said Jimmy.

"I know," said Juggins. "Hold tight!"

As they went over the highest rocks, they could look across the island to the deserted fisherman's hut. There was no breeze today, so the old door was not flapping about. But just as Juggins and Jimmy looked at it, it was suddenly pushed open from the inside, and a man walked out. Juggins caught her breath.

"It's Buck Carter!" she said. Juggins and Jimmy never knew how they got back to the *Pea Pod*. Not daring to look behind them to see if Buck Carter was coming, they stumbled along over the loose stones of the beach, carrying the struggling seal.

The seal did not seem to be as frightened now, but it was a very slippery little animal, and Juggins and Jimmy had to hold it tightly with both hands. At last they came in sight of the *Pea Pod*, and Juggins stopped short.

"There's another boat on the beach," she said. "What if it's Buck Carter's!" But it wasn't. It was Mr. Ted's. He and Miss Cherry were just coming around the end of a big rock, and Mr. Ted was carrying a picnic basket.

"Oh, thank goodness," exclaimed Juggins. As soon as Jimmy saw them, he was so glad that he dropped the tail of the little seal and ran to meet them. And as soon as he dropped the tail, the little animal began to slip, slip, slip, through Juggins's arms.

"Oh, somebody come quick!" she cried as she stood still

in the middle of the beach, holding on as hard as she could. Mr. Ted hurried toward Juggins.

"What on earth–!" he began. Then he ran quickly and caught the seal, just as its round head was slipping through Juggins's hands. Juggins took hold of its tail and together they put the seal safely into the bottom of the *Pea Pod*.

After Juggins and Jimmy had told Mr. Ted and Miss Cherry all about the seals, Mr. Ted pushed the *Pea Pod* into the water and helped Juggins and Jimmy get in. Then he pushed them off, and he and Miss Cherry watched and waved while Juggins rowed up the harbor. There was no mist now, and the fog had gone far out to sea.

"We didn't see the Red Robber at all," said Juggins, very disappointed. "We will have to come again." She looked down at the bottom of the boat, where the little seal was flopping about from one side to the other, and she smiled a little. "But we found something else," she said.

"Do you think we should name it?" asked Jimmy.

"Yes," said Juggins, and she stopped rowing and leaned on her oars for a moment, while she thought about all the names she knew. Finally she said, "We could call it 'Little Orphan Annie.'" And so they did.

SEVERAL THINGS HAPPEN

*L*ittle Orphan Annie spent the night in the bottom of the *Pea Pod.* And the first thing the next morning Juggins and Jimmy went fishing and caught six cunners for her breakfast. When they put the cunners into the *Pea Pod*, Little Orphan Annie gobbled them up right away, heads, tails, fins, and all. But she did not seem very happy. She sat at one side of the boat, with her little round head just above the edge, and looked at the water. Whenever Juggins and Jimmy came near the *Pea Pod*, she flopped about so much that they were afraid she would flop right over the side.

"Perhaps she wants a drink," said Jimmy.

So Juggins brought a pan of nice cool water from the little green pump. Little Orphan Annie could not tell them that she did not like fresh water, but the next time she flopped, she flopped right into the pan, and upset the water all over the inside of the boat.

"Never mind," said Juggins. "She likes sitting where it's wet anyway."

"We could bring her some seaweed to sit on," said Jimmy.

So they ran down to the rocks at the edge of the water and brought armfuls of dripping seaweed to make a nice bed for her. But poor Little Orphan Annie just flopped under a seat at the other end of the boat.

All day long Juggins and Jimmy trotted back and forth, trying to make Little Orphan Annie happy. They gathered snails, and dug them out of the shells for her, but she just turned her head away when they held them up in front of her nose. They brought many small stones and put them under the seaweed to make it seem more like Mad Cap Island. Then they caught some more cunners for her which she gobbled up. But still she looked unhappy.

Late in the afternoon, Mr. Ted and Miss Cherry came with some friends to visit her. But she just lay in the bottom of the *Pea Pod* and looked at them with her big round sad eyes. It had been a very exciting and busy day for Juggins and Jimmy. And it was not until Jimmy had gone home, and Juggins had said good night to Little Orphan Annie and come in for supper, that she noticed Father's eyes. There was no twinkle in them at all, in fact they looked as sad as Little Orphan Annie's.

"Oh, dear," thought Juggins. She had never seen Father look like this before. Could it be that he had heard about the dreadful thing Buck Carter had said? Father never talked very much, but tonight he hardly said a word until they had finished their supper. Then he said something so nice that Juggins felt better.

"Some of the lobster traps need to be repaired," he said. "Tomorrow we'll bring them in and we'll bring in the lobster buoys, too, and give them a fresh coat of paint."

"Oh, boy," said Juggins. It was fun having her lobster buoy children come home to be painted. She liked to help Father put them into new yellow jackets, and after they were all freshly painted, and before they went back into the ocean, she would give them a party.

The next morning Juggins got up very early, so that she would have time to give Little Orphan Annie her breakfast of cunners, and bring her fresh seaweed before Father was ready to go out in the dory.

Little Orphan Annie did not flop quite so much this morning, and Juggins thought that she must be getting used to her new home. But she did still look sad. Juggins waved to her as she and Father rowed off down the harbor to get the lobster traps.

When they came back, they brought eight of the lobster buoy children with them. There was no fog this morning, and no Red Robber to be looked for. The ocean was a beautiful clear blue, and the sun was so bright it made Juggins's eyes squint. She could not help feeling happy as she rode home in the dory on top of the lobster traps, with her smiling children all around her.

After lunch she and Father put a bench outside the house, and set up the lobster buoy children all in a row. Then they went into the shed, and Father passed the cans of paint down from the shelf to Juggins.

"There's lots of yellow," said Juggins, looking into the cans, "but there's hardly any red. Should we give the children blue grins?" she asked.

"We'll see," said Father.

They each took a brush and set to work. Father could paint faster than Juggins, because his brush was so much bigger. But she did Tiny Tim and Mr. Hoover all by herself. Father put painted buttons on the front of his jackets, and they looked very nice, but Juggins just made a blue line up and down Tiny Tim's and Mr. Hoover's jackets.

"They're zipper jackets," said Juggins, as she looked at Father's puzzled expression.

"Of course," said Father, laughing. "I should have known."

When the lobster buoy children were all bright and shining in their new clothes, Father mixed a little turpentine with the red paint, and there was enough after all, to give everyone a grin from ear to ear. Tiny Tim and Mr. Hoover grinned more than the others–but then, their jackets zipped!

After Father had put away the paints, and gone down to his lobster traps on the float, Juggins stood in front of her lobster buoy children and thought about Geraldine. What had Buck Carter done with poor Geraldine? Was she lying, battered and all alone, somewhere off on the rocks? Would she ever again have a bright yellow jacket and a happy red smile like the others? Juggins's lower lip started to quiver and her eyes filled up as she thought about her special Geraldine.

When she turned to go into The Barnacle, she saw Jimmy coming down the path through the wildflowers and lupine. He was running as fast as he could in his cork jacket, and he was waving something white. Juggins ran out into the road to meet him.

"What's that?" she asked, looking at the envelope in Jimmy's hand.

"Grandmother's written something about the Red Robber.

I've got to take it to the constable's house," said Jimmy, look-
ing very important. "Can you come with me?" "To Jasper
Beach's?" said Juggins. She had never in her life been to
Jasper Beach's door, except with Father.

"Yes," said Jimmy. "It's about catching the Red Robber. I
guess they'll get him now."

"All right," said Juggins, "I'll go with you." She would do
anything to catch the Red Robber.

So she and Jimmy walked along the road, past all the
fishermen's houses, until they came to the constable's house.
Jasper Beach was not sitting on his porch today, so they tiptoed slowly up the gravel walk and knocked softly at the
kitchen door. Nobody came, and they knocked again. They
had to knock four times before they heard heavy footsteps
coming toward the door. It was suddenly opened wide, and
there stood Jasper Beach himself. He was very tall, with a big,
round stomach, and he looked down at Juggins and Jimmy
over his spectacles, and grunted. But he did not speak.

"Hello," said Jimmy, looking all the way up to Jasper
Beach's face, and not feeling quite so important. "Grandmother sent this for you," and he held out the envelope.

Jasper Beach grunted again and took it from Jimmy's
hand.

"Goodbye," said Jimmy quickly, and he turned and ran
away as fast as he could.

But Juggins did not move from the doorstep. She had not
heard a word that Jimmy had said, and she was staring right
past Jasper Beach into his house. For there, standing on
Jasper Beach's kitchen mantel, beside his clock, was–what do
you think? Geraldine!!

In a moment the door was closed again, and Juggins was

running after Jimmy, to tell him what she had seen. Although they talked about Geraldine all the way back to the field path, neither of them could figure out what she could possibly be doing in Jasper Beach's kitchen.

When Juggins came to The Barnacle, Father was leaning on the lobster sign waiting for her. She stood beside him as four fishermen went by on their way home from Back Cove.

"Hello," said Father, to the fishermen. "Hello," said Juggins, too, for she knew them all. But the fishermen did not say hello, or even look at Father and Juggins. They just walked along down the road as if they hadn't even seen them. Juggins looked after them in astonishment. Then she looked up

at Father's eyes and she knew. The fishermen all believed that Father–*her* Father–was the Red Robber, and they would not speak to him anymore.

"Who's going to get supper?" asked Father, putting his arm around Juggins's shoulders. But Juggins turned away and ran fast into The Barnacle.

When Father came into the kitchen, there was no one putting the kettle on for tea, or bringing the bread from the cupboard. Juggins was on her little bed in the other room with her face buried deep in the patchwork quilt.

A PARTY FOR ALL

When Juggins came out into the kitchen the next morning, Father was not there, but a bowl of cereal and a cup of milk were waiting for her on the table. Father always left them there when he had to leave early. He must have thought of Little Orphan Annie, too, because there were three cunners in a pan on the doorstep. Before Juggins sat down to eat her breakfast, she took the cunners out of the pan, and ran down the rocky path to the float.

Little Orphan Annie did not flop around at all when Juggins climbed into the *Pea Pod*, and she gobbled up the cunners in no time. Her eyes seemed bigger and rounder than ever. Juggins thought she looked a little sad and lonesome sitting all by herself in the bottom of the boat.

"I want you to be happy," said Juggins, out loud. So she gathered some fresh seaweed with a live crab in it and put it in front of Little Orphan Annie's nose. Then Juggins ran back up to the house and sat down at the kitchen table to eat her own breakfast.

She wondered where Father was. Perhaps he had gone to find Barney. Barney was their best friend, and he would surely tell everyone that Father was not the Red Robber. She hoped Barney would come back with Father, because Barney

79

always made her feel happy. And Juggins was feeling a little sad and lonesome herself as she sat all alone in The Barnacle.

She looked out the kitchen window toward the road, but all she saw was the quiet morning mist. Suddenly, she thought she saw something move out by the board sign and, then, she heard a familiar voice.

"Go home," said the voice. "Go home, go home!" it said, this time very loud.

Juggins ran to the door, and there was Jimmy coming around the side of the house with a small basket in his hand. He was shaking the basket at Tansey, who was following behind.

"Go home!" said Jimmy, again. But Tansey, who always did exactly what he liked, had no idea of going home. Instead, he scampered off through the tall grass after a cricket.

"Look," said Jimmy, holding out the basket for Juggins to see. "I picked them in Grandmother's garden. They're for you."

"Oh," said Juggins, looking in, "I love them." The basket was chockful of big red raspberries which were Juggins's favorite.

"Let's put them in two bowls with milk and sugar," said Jimmy.

"No," said Juggins, "I have a better idea. We'll put them in the sea urchin cups and have a party, and the lobster buoy children can come if they are dry."

"All right!" said Jimmy, as he and Juggins went to the bench where the lobster buoy children were all standing in a row. They felt their jackets and, sure enough, the paint had dried. As Juggins looked down the rocky path, and through the mist, she could just barely see the *Pea Pod* rocking back and forth against the float.

"I wish Little Orphan Annie could come, too," said Juggins. "I think she needs a party." "Then let's have the party down on the float," said Jimmy.

"Good idea," said Juggins. She and Jimmy carried the lobster buoy children two by two by their rope hair down to the float. They set them up in a circle as near to the *Pea Pod* as possible. Then Juggins brought the little sea urchin cups and they filled them with the raspberries. There were exactly eight, so they put one in front of each lobster buoy child. There was a big old lobster that Father had left in a pail on the float, and Juggins thought he should come to the party, too. So she turned the pail upside down, and sat the lobster on top of it, right between two of the lobster buoy children. Jimmy was not sure that he liked this new guest, for he looked very much like grandfather lobster.

"There aren't any raspberries for him," said Jimmy.

"We can give him some fish bait," said Juggins. She took a piece of fish out of the bucket that was in the dory and put it on top of the pail in front of old Mr. Lobster.

"There, now he's all set," she said.

When Juggins turned around, she saw Tansey who had wandered curiously down to the float to see what all the activity was about. Juggins quickly caught him and put him on another upturned pail. Then she put a small handful of the fish bait in front of him. Tansey took one sniff of the bait, jumped off the pail tipping it over, and ran away from the party as fast as he could.

"I guess Tansey doesn't like parties," said Jimmy, picking up the pail.

"I think he only likes fresh caught cunners," said Juggins.

"I wish Little Orphan Annie could come up here on the float," said Jimmy. "She can't see very well from down there."

Juggins looked at Little Orphan Annie sitting on the seaweed in the bottom of the *Pea Pod*. Then she looked at the end of the float, where Father's half-mended lobster traps lay scattered about.

"I know," said Juggins. "We can take her out of the boat and put her under a lobster trap. Then she can see everything." They picked out the biggest of the traps and dragged it over beside the *Pea Pod*.

"Father has taken the old broken slats off the bottom," said Juggins, "so Little Orphan Annie will fit in perfectly."

Then Juggins got into the boat and, while Jimmy stood ready with the trap, she clasped Little Orphan Annie tightly around the middle and lifted her—PLOP—out onto the float. Then, down—SLAM—went the lobster trap over her and there was Little Orphan Annie looking out with frightened eyes through the slits of her new cage.

Now, just as the party was about to begin, Juggins thought of something else and she ran up the rocky path into the house. When she came out, she was carrying the red silk sash of her Sunday dress.

"Little Orphan Annie ought to have something festive on for the party," said Juggins, and while Jimmy lifted up the lobster trap, she tied the red sash around Annie's neck and under her chin. "There, she's all ready," said Juggins.

Jimmy then got another piece of fish bait from the dory and put it in the lobster trap–and now the party really began!

Juggins and Jimmy sat down in the circle and helped the lobster buoy children eat their raspberries out of the sea urchin cups. Little Orphan Annie, who did not like being dressed up, flopped around under the lobster trap and behaved very badly. But then, it was her first party. And old Mr. Lobster seemed very content sitting on his pail sniffing the fish bait.

When the raspberries were almost eaten up, Jimmy suddenly pointed to the rocks along the shore and cried, "Tansey's going into the ocean!"

Sure enough, there was Tansey on the edge of the rocks, dabbling for something in the water with his paw.

Juggins and Jimmy jumped up and ran as fast as they could along the shore to the rescue. But Tansey did not want to be rescued and, as soon as he saw Juggins and Jimmy coming, he went bounding away over the slippery rocks. Tansey came fishing by himself nearly every day and he was quite used to slippery rocks. However, Jimmy was not and suddenly his feet went out from under him. Down he slid over the wet seaweed and, with a splash, landed right in the water with his cork jacket.

"Oh, oh!" yelled Jimmy.

"Oh, no!" cried Juggins

But Jimmy did not go very far, and the water was not at all deep.

"I don't float!" yelled Jimmy, holding tight to the seaweed.

"You can't," said Juggins, laughing, "because you're standing up." Then she grabbed hold of his hand and pulled him safely back on the rocks. Now, Jimmy was not only very wet, but also a little scared, and he didn't want any more party.

"I'm going back to Grandmother's," he said, with a shaky voice, as he started to run toward the path.

Juggins watched him scamper off, and as she came around the corner of The Barnacle, she heard a strange banging sound down on the float. Father, who was sitting on the doorstep mending a lobster trap, heard it, too. He and Juggins both started down the rocky path to see what was the matter. Exciting things were going on at the party. Old Mr. Lobster had fallen off his pail, and he was knocking the little sea urchin cups about with his claws. And Little Orphan Annie's lobster trap was jumping up and down on the float. Inside it poor Annie was hung up by her necktie on a nail. She was choking and struggling to get free.

"Oh, dear," cried Juggins, as she lifted up the trap. Father quickly unhooked Little Orphan Annie and took off her necktie and put it in his pocket. Juggins held her tight to the float, while Father gently felt around her throat with his fingers.

"She will be all right," he said, after a few moments.

"Are you very sure," asked Juggins, still a bit worried.

"I'm sure," said Father, as he pulled the nail out of the

trap. Then Juggins carefully lowered the trap back over Little Orphan Annie.

"I'm sorry," she said, looking at Annie through the slats. "Now, please don't flop around any-more, or I'll have to put you right to bed in the *Pea Pod!*"

But when Little Orphan Annie's bedtime came that night, she slept quietly under her new cage.

SOMETHING IN A SHELL

*T*he next morning Father did not say a word all the time he and Juggins were eating their breakfast. And as soon as they had finished, he went out the kitchen door looking very gloomy. Juggins did not like to see Father looking so sad. He must be worried about the Red Robber, she thought as she sat down on the doorstep to wait for Jimmy. But Jimmy did not come and, after a while, Juggins began to feel a little sad and lonesome again.

Then all of a sudden she had a thought. She would go to see Mrs. Milly Willy and take her the overalls that Father had left on the chair, because they needed a patch. Mrs. Milly Willy was a very cheerful person to go to visit, and she knew a great deal about patching.

Juggins could sew on buttons quite nicely for Father, but sometimes her patches looked a little peculiar. So she took the overalls and started off along the road that led to the end of the harbor. Perhaps I'll meet Father, or Mr. Ted, or some-body, thought Juggins. But there was nobody to be seen on the road, or around the fishermen's cottages.

When she came to the constable's house, she thought about poor Geraldine and wondered if she was still standing up on the mantel beside the kitchen clock. Jasper Beach was not sitting on his porch today, but there was a white card stuck on the outside of his gate with a thumbtack. Juggins stopped to see what was printed on the card, and this is what she read:

$200 Reward

will be paid to the person
who discovers and identifies the
robber who is stealing lobsters
from the Seal Harbor traps.

Elizabeth Crabtree
Jasper Beach

Juggins was sure that this must be what Jimmy had brought in the envelope to Jasper Beach from his grandmother. She spelled out the long words to herself several times.

She did not know what they all meant, but Jimmy had said his grandmother was going to give a lot of money to catch the Red Robber, and this card must be about that. Juggins stared at the figures at the top and wondered how a person who had $200 would really feel. Probably everyone would try to catch the Red Robber now, she thought. Maybe they were all out looking for him in the fog, and would find him this very afternoon. At least then if someone caught him, everyone would know it wasn't Father who was stealing the lobsters. Thinking about all of this made Juggins feel happier as she skipped along the road to Mrs. Milly Willy's store.

There was no one in the store except Muffin and her kittens. The little fluff balls had their eyes open now, and they were crawling around the floor. Juggins patted them and told them that she would bring more cunners very soon.

Then she looked through the door behind the counter that led into the small kitchen, and there was Mrs. Milly Willy in a purple-flowered dress, sitting at the table, working on her hooked rug. Even on foggy days, Mrs. Milly Willy's kitchen seemed full of sunshine, for there was golden glow growing outside both of the windows and her two yellow canaries were always singing in their cages.

When it was damp, Mrs. Milly Willy liked to make herself a cup of hot tea, and Juggins could see the shiny copper tea kettle whistling away on the stove.

Juggins stood in the doorway, holding the overalls behind her back.

"Hello," she said.

"Well, Lord love a duck!" said Mrs. Milly Willy, looking up with a smile all over her round, merry face. "Whatever do you want in my store?"

"It begins with a P," said Juggins, smiling back. This was a game that Juggins and Mrs. Milly Willy played together very often.

"Potatoes," said Mrs. Milly Willy.

"No," said Juggins, shaking her head.

"Pumpkin pies," said Mrs. Milly Willy.

"No," said Juggins, shaking her head again.

"Prunes and pickled pigs feet," said Mrs. Milly Willy.

"No," said Juggins, shaking her head harder than ever.

"I give up," said Mrs. Milly Willy. Then Juggins held Father's overalls up in front of her, so Mrs. Milly Willy could see the big hole in the knee. "Patch!" cried Mrs. Milly Willy. "Yes," said Juggins. And they both laughed.

Mrs. Milly Willy got up from her chair and walked across the kitchen into the closet where her ragbag hung.

Juggins thought that Mrs. Milly Willy's ragbag must be a magic one, because whenever she put her hand into it, a piece of cloth just the right color always came out. And sure enough, when Mrs. Milly Willy came back across the kitchen, she had a square of overall blue denim in her hand. Juggins sat down on a chair next to Mrs. Milly Willy and watched her set and baste the patch on the overalls with her plump fingers.

"Now you must sew it yourself," said Mrs. Milly Willy, "while I make the tea."

So Juggins took the overalls and Mrs. Milly Willy's thimble and, with the heels of her sandals on the rung of the chair, she began to sew around the patch. She did not get along very fast because, after every few stitches, the big thimble dropped off her finger down onto the floor, and she would have to stop and get it again.

When Mrs. Milly Willy had made the tea, she came back and sat in her chair next to Juggins.

"Did you like to sew patches when you were a little girl?" asked Juggins, with a sigh, as she went after the thimble for the sixth time.

"No," said Mrs. Milly Willy, sipping her tea, "but I wasn't even seven years old when I set my first patch."

"All by yourself?" asked Juggins, looking astonished.

"Yes," said Mrs. Milly Willy, with a chuckle, "and I got sent to bed for it, too."

"Why?" asked Juggins, looking at Mrs. Milly Willy instead of at the patch. She never could remember to keep on sewing when Mrs. Milly Willy began to tell a story.

"Well," began Mrs. Milly Willy, "it was my old Aunt Cornelia who taught me to sew when I was a very little child.

90

She was most strict, and I was a willful young one that would run away from my sewing whenever I could. One day I heard Aunt tell my father that if I lived to be a hundred, she was sure I would not have to mend his clothes, because I could never sew all around a patch without running away.

"Now there wasn't anything I wouldn't do for my father, small as I was. So that afternoon, when I found his old jeans on a chair with a hole in the knee, I thought I would show him that I could make a patch all by myself. But I had nothing to make a patch with, and Aunt Cornelia kept her ragbag locked up in her own closet. I tried to think of where I could get some cloth, when I suddenly saw my apron hanging on a hook beside the closet door. I didn't think Aunt would notice if one of the apron strings was a little shorter than the other, so I got the scissors and cut off a good size piece on one of the ends.

"My apron was pink, but I set the piece on father's jeans as straight as I could.

"Then I sewed it round and round and round, until my little fingers were all pricked up. And as funny as it looked on father's old blue jeans, I thought the patch was beautiful. And I forgot that nobody could help seeing the patch, even if they didn't notice the apron strings! Well, Aunt Cornelia's sharp eyes were the very first to see it, and off I went to bed without any supper. Because Aunt was upset with me for ruining my apron."

Juggins's eyes grew wide as she listened to Mrs. Milly Willy, and she was no longer sewing her patch. Mrs. Milly Willy continued. "But while I was lying on my bed crying, up came father, secret-like. He was carrying a small tray and, on the tray, was a popover and a cup of warm milk."

"Oh," said Juggins, interrupting, "when you were a little girl did you like popovers as much as I do?"

"Yes," said Mrs. Milly Willy, "especially with strawberry jam!"

Juggins knew it was not polite to interrupt when someone was talking, but she couldn't help it, as she was thinking how good one of Mrs. Milly Willy's popovers would taste right this very minute.

"Now," said Mrs. Milly Willy, "father sat down on the edge of my bed and told me how much he liked the patch, and how nicely he thought I had sewed it on. This made me feel better and I stopped crying. Then father said if I would be a good girl and mind Aunt, then the next time he went to Boston in the schooner, he would bring me something special."

"Did he?" asked Juggins.

"Yes," said Mrs. Milly Willy, "and it was something so special that after that I could finish a patch without once putting it down."

"What was it?" asked Juggins.

Mrs. Milly Willy smiled at Juggins again, and with a twinkle in her eye she said, "It begins with T."

"Tea set," guessed Juggins.

"No," said Mrs. Milly Willy.

Juggins wrinkled her forehead and thought for a moment, but she could not think of any other special thing that began with a T.

"I give up," said Juggins.

"Oh, no," said Mrs. Milly Willy, shaking her finger at Juggins. But then she put down her cup of tea, and walked over to the closet. She opened the door and took something out of a box which was on the top shelf.

"If I let you look at it, will you finish your patch?" asked Mrs. Milly Willy.

"Oh, yes, I will," answered Juggins.

So Mrs. Milly Willy opened her hand and there was a little double shell, with a hinge on one edge and a hook on the other.

"But shell begins with an S," said Juggins.

"Look inside," said Mrs. Milly Willy, handing Juggins the shell. Juggins carefully unfastened the little hook.

"Thimble!" she cried. And there it was–a very small shiny silver thimble in a nest of red velvet. Juggins thought it was prettier than anything she had ever seen.

"Can I put it on, Mrs. Milly Willy?" asked Juggins.

"Sure you can," said Mrs. Milly Willy, as she went out into the store to wait on a customer.

Juggins put the silver thimble on her finger, and it fit as if it had been bought for her instead of for the little Milly who did not like to sew patches, either. Then she picked up Father's overalls and began to make stitches as fast as she could. The little thimble did not drop off at all. And she finished her patch in a very few minutes.

When she was done, Juggins did not want to take the thimble off, because it looked so nice on her finger. But after looking at it for a minute, she put it carefully away in the shell and hooked the hook. Then she went out into the store and found Mrs. Milly Willy sitting behind the counter.

"Shall I put the thimble back on the shelf?" asked Juggins.

"No," said Mrs. Milly Willy.

So Juggins put it on the counter, and gave Mrs. Milly Willy the overalls. Mrs. Milly Willy looked them over, and seemed to like the patch, for she nodded her head. And without saying a word, she opened the glass candy case and took out a gumdrop that she popped right into Juggins's mouth.

Then she folded the overalls and put the shell with the little thimble into one of the pockets!

"We must push it way down in," said Mrs. Milly Willy, "so it won't fall out on your way home."

"I'm going to take it home?" asked Juggins, looking up at Mrs. Milly Willy with her round, shining eyes.

"Yes, now run along," said Mrs. Milly Willy, as she leaned over and kissed Juggins on the top of her head.

"Oh, thank you, Mrs. Milly Willy," said Juggins. And out the door she ran because she had to find Father, as soon as she could, to show him the new patch and the very special silver thimble.

It Looks Like Tom

When Juggins came out of Mrs. Milly Willy's store, she could see that there were some fishermen gathered around Barney's new boat in the open shed at the edge of the harbor. The mist was too thick for her to see who the fishermen were, but she thought one of them might be Father. Tightly holding the overalls with the precious thimble tucked inside the pocket, she ran down over the grassy hill to find him.

But when she got to the shed and looked in, she did not see Father or Barney. The other fishermen were walking around the boat, running their hands over its curving sides, and rapping it here and there with their knuckles. One of them said it was the finest boat he had ever seen.

Juggins thought so, too. It was all painted now, gleaming white, with a band of blue around the edge, and up in the prow Barney had put a small carved figure with its arms stretched out toward the sea.

"Oh," gasped Juggins, under her breath when she saw it. She thought that it looked just like a real mermaid and she tiptoed around behind the fishermen so she could get a closer look. And then she saw something else. On the side of the boat right under the figure, Barney had painted the name: Jolly Jimmy.

Juggins spelled out the words, and thought about Jimmy. Wouldn't he be happy, his own name on this wonderful new boat! She ran her fingers along the letters also painted blue, and tried to reach up and touch the white figure. But her arms were too short. All of a sudden she heard Barney's voice behind her and, when she turned around, there was Father, too. She was so glad to see him that, this time, she did not notice that none of the fishermen spoke to him; although they all said hello to Barney.

"Oh, Father," cried Juggins, running to him and holding out the overalls, "see the patch I made for you, and see what Mrs. Milly Willy gave me." She put her hand into the pocket of the overalls and felt around for the shell. But Mrs. Milly Willy had pushed it down very deep and Juggins had trouble reaching it. When she finally pulled it out, she also pulled out the red silk sash of her Sunday dress, which Father had stuffed into the pocket after he had taken it from Little Orphan Annie's neck. Juggins threw the sash over the edge of the boat, and held out the little shell for Father to see.

"Look," she began excitedly, "it opens like–." And then she suddenly stopped, for Father was not looking at her or at the shell. He was looking straight at the fishermen on the other side of the boat, and the fishermen were all staring at her red sash. For a few moments no one spoke and Father, and everyone else, had strange looks on their faces. Juggins was sure that something dreadful was going to happen, and she took hold of Father's hand and squeezed it tight.

Finally, one of the fishermen shrugged his shoulders and sighed. "It looks like Tom all right," he said, pointing his finger at the red sash.

"Right out of his own pocket, too," said another fisherman.

Juggins stared at the sash and then at the fishermen. What did they mean? Then Barney, who was standing on the other side of Father, spoke.

"You boys are crazy," said Barney, bringing his fist down hard on the edge of the boat.

"You ought to know that's the sash of a child's dress, not the Red Robber's scarf, and you ought to know that Tom Tibbetts would never touch a lobster that didn't belong to him.

""Oh, yeah?" said a third fisherman. "Well, I'll tell you that the robber was seen out there this morning in the fog. And he had on a scarf just like that one." And, as he pointed to the sash, he added, "Did anyone see Tom around anywhere early this morning?" The other fishermen all shook their heads.

"And the robber comes in a dory," said a fourth fisherman. "Is there anyone else here who still goes out to sea in a dory except Tom Tibbetts?" The fishermen shook their heads again.

"And Jasper Beach has a lobster buoy over at his house that belongs to Tom," said the first fisherman. "It was picked up the other day floating just where the traps had been robbed. Jasper has been keeping it 'til we find more evidence –and I guess we've found it now. You'd better come along with us over to Jasper's, Tom!"

Juggins, feeling terribly frightened, had been looking from one to the other while holding tight to Father's hand. Suddenly she forgot to be afraid.

"That is my sash," she said, stamping her sandal on the floor of the shed, looking right over the boat at the fishermen, "and my Father is not the Red Robber." After she said this, Father looked down at her for the first time and said, "Sara Belle, I want you to run along home now. I will come in a little while."

Now Juggins was more frightened than ever, for Father looked very grim, and he never called her Sara Belle unless he was most displeased. A long time ago, when she was little and had cut a new fish net with a knife, he had called her that. Juggins thought that Father looked now exactly the way he had looked that day, and so she let go of his hand and walked slowly out of the shed, across the grass. She did not want to go back to The Barnacle alone, and leave Father with these cruel fishermen. And as she walked along, her eyes began to fill with tears. She could hardly see where she was going, and there was an awful lump in her throat that she kept trying to swallow. But she walked straight ahead, and did not turn around until she came to the road. She was afraid she might see them taking Father to the constable's.

When she was in front of Mrs. Milly Willy's store, she wiped her eyes on her sleeve and looked back quickly toward the shed. The men were still all around the boat, and Barney was standing close to Father. That made Juggins feel a little better, but the lump in her throat was still there.

As she ran on, she did not see Mrs. Milly Willy out behind the store feeding her chickens, or Mr. Ted and Miss Cherry waving to her from the field. She did not even notice that she had left Father's overalls and the precious shell behind in the shed. It was hours before she thought of her

101

little silver thimble again, because of all the things that continued to happen this strange afternoon.

When Juggins came to the high place in the road just beyond Jasper Beach's, the fog was not quite so thick. Over the roofs of the other fishermen's houses, she could see The Barnacle and the float at the edge of the harbor.

And as she looked at the float, she saw something that made her stand still right in the middle of the road. Jimmy was down on the float in his cork jacket, and he had taken the big old lobster trap off from over Little Orphan Annie. And he was trying to lift her back into the *Pea Pod*.

Juggins knew it was hard enough for two people to hold Little Orphan Annie, but for one person, with a cork jacket sticking out in front, it was impossible. Jimmy's fingers barely went around Little Orphan Annie's middle and Juggins, although far away on the road, could see her begin to slip, slip, slip through his arms. Jimmy clutched and clutched, but it was of no use. Little Orphan Annie went right on slipping, until she slipped–PLOP–right out of his arms and off the float into the water.

In a moment she was swimming away, her little gray head bobbing on top of the waves. Juggins did not wait to see what Jimmy did next. She ran like mad down the hill and along the road to The Barnacle. When she came around the corner in sight of the float again, guess what else had happened.

THE RED ROBBER AT LAST

Jimmy had gone after Little Orphan Annie in the *Pea Pod*! When Juggins came running down the rocky path, he was already far out from the float, and he had lost one of the oars overboard. Juggins could still see Little Orphan Annie's round head swimming away into the fog, but Jimmy was not catching up with her. He was sitting in the middle seat, trying to row with one oar, and the *Pea Pod* was just going around and around in circles.

"Paddle back here," shouted Juggins.

"I can't," Jimmy shouted back. "The boat doesn't work."

Juggins could see that the *Pea Pod* was beginning to drift down the harbor. The tide was running out very fast, and although Jimmy kept going around and around in circles, he went farther and father away into the fog. Juggins could just barely see him, one oar going up and down like the arm of a windmill.

"Oh, dear!" cried Juggins, jumping up and down. "What should I do?" Somebody must go after Jimmy right away, she thought, but who? She looked up at the road and along the shore and, although she could not see very far because of the fog, there was not a person in sight. And she knew Father and Barney were too far away to help. Then she looked at the dory.

105

Juggins had never in her life been out in the dory all by herself, because Father said that it was much to heavy for her to row. But by now Jimmy and the *Pea Pod* had drifted so far into the fog that she could no longer see them at all. I'll have to go, she thought, and she ran over to the dory and began to untie it as fast she she could. The big rope was heavy and wet, and it seemed as if the knot would never come loose. But at last it did, and Juggins jumped into the dory and pushed it away from the float. Luckily, Father had left the oars in the boat and, in a minute, Juggins was standing up in the middle, just the way Father did, rowing slowly out into the harbor. The oars were big and hard to lift, but she remembered what Father had said about all Tibbettses having strong muscles in their arms to row with. She pushed and pulled and her face got hotter and her breath got shorter as she rowed along.

"Jimmy," she shouted between strokes. "Where are you? I'm coming in the dory." Somewhere in the fog she could hear Jimmy calling:

"I'm over here."

Soon Juggins had rowed so far out into the harbor that the dory began to drift with the tide, too, and she rowed much easier and faster. Then, suddenly, through the fog she saw the outline of the *Pea Pod*, and Jimmy still splashing the oar up and down. In a few minutes the dory and the *Pea Pod* were side by side.

"You must get in here," said Juggins, and she leaned over and held the two boats together while Jimmy carefully climbed up into the dory.

Now Jimmy, feeling safer in the bigger boat with Juggins, sat down on the bow seat and hugged the cork jacket tightly around himself. He did not move a muscle as he watched Juggins tie the rope from the *Pea Pod* to the end of the dory, so they could tow it home.

When Juggins picked up the oars and started to row again, Jimmy said, "I wonder where Little Orphan Annie is. I think she went that way," he said, pointing his finger. Juggins stopped rowing and looked all around in the circle of fog, but as far as she could see there was no little gray head swimming on the water.

"We can't go out any farther in the fog," she said. "It's coming in thicker than ever. I guess we'll have to go home."

She did want to find Little Orphan Annie, but she knew the danger of going into the fog. So she began to row again toward the float. It was harder now, because she had to row against the tide. Juggins pulled and pulled at the oars, while Jimmy sat on the opposite seat, and looked back over the water for Little Orphan Annie.

"You're face is awf'ly red," said Jimmy, after a few minutes.

Juggins dropped one of the oars and wiped her forehead, and when she stopped rowing she heard a sound that made her very worried. It was the sound of waves off to one side, breaking on the rocks. Juggins knew that they must be the rocks of Mad Cap Island. The dory had drifted to the very mouth of the harbor, and the strong tide was carrying them out to sea faster than she could row the boat toward home. Now that she was not rowing, Juggins could see how swiftly the tide was running and taking the dory with it. She also knew that was how Mad Cap got its name–the tide rushed so madly by the island on its way out.

Quickly Juggins picked up the oars again and pulled with all her might. Her face grew hotter and redder than ever, as she tried to force the heavy dory against the tide. She could not see the shore because of the fog, so she was not sure whether they were going ahead, but after a few minutes, she could hear the waves breaking now back where they had come from, instead of off to one side. Despite her efforts, the dory had drifted right out into the open ocean, beyond Mad Cap Island.

"When are we going to get home?" asked Jimmy, holding on to the sides of the dory, for the sea was rougher now.

"I don't know," said Juggins, her heart beating fast, as she struggled with the oars.

She had given up trying to row the dory ahead, and all she wanted to do now was to keep it pointed into the waves so that the water would not come over the sides of the boat.

Juggins was used to being out on the ocean, and she was not very much afraid except of the fog. Perhaps some fisherman would come along soon and pick them up, she thought. If only the fog would go out, someone would be sure to see them right away. She listened for the sound of a motor somewhere in the mist, but she heard none. Maybe when the tide turned she would be able to row in herself. And she hoped that it would turn before they had drifted too far, because her arms were tired, and it was a little scary out there along with Jimmy in the fog.

Suddenly she saw a small yellow spot floating on top of a wave, and then she saw another and another.

"Oh, look!" exclaimed Juggins, as she saw her own lobster buoy children dancing merrily on top of the water. It did not seem so far away from home now with all her family around. Jimmy did not see the lobster buoy children because

108

he was looking the other way. He quickly stood up in the middle of the dory.

"There's something moving out there. Look. I see someone," he said, pointing in the other direction.

Juggins turned and saw that there was a boat quite close to them in the mist. It was another dory, and the fisherman in it was just leaning over to pull in a lobster trap.

"He's pulling one of our traps!" whispered Juggins in surprise and fear. And sure enough, on the end of the rope that he was pulling was a lobster buoy with a bright yellow jacket and a big wide grin.

The fisherman stood up straight in his dory, with the lobster trap in his arms, and Juggins and Jimmy both shrieked right out loud, for around the fisherman's neck and up to his ears was a bright red scarf!

It was the Red Robber!

Startled by the sounds and commotion behind him, the fisherman dropped the lobster trap back into the water with a splash. And as he bent over to reach for the oars, the scarf slipped slightly revealing more of his face. He did not look to see who was behind him, as he quickly started rowing away as fast as he could.

Just for a moment Juggins and Jimmy had seen the face behind the scarf and they shrieked again, for they knew who the Red Robber was!

ADRIFT

The face that Juggins and Jimmy saw hidden behind the red scarf was the squinty, scowly face of Buck Carter. Buck Carter was the Red Robber!

Juggins and Jimmy were so surprised that for a moment they almost forgot where they were. But when the other dory moved quickly away into the mist, Juggins suddenly felt very afraid. And she was much more afraid of the fog than she was of the Red Robber.

"Buck Carter," she called as loud as she could, "we can't row in. Oh, Buck, won't you please take us home." But the Red Robber was gone. He had slipped silently away into the fog, without once looking around. Juggins began to row as hard as she could toward the spot where the other dory had disappeared.

"Oh, Buck!" she cried, again, with a little sob, "come back. Oh, please come back and help us!"

When Jimmy realized that Juggins was frightened, he began to be frightened, too.

"I, I, I want to go home," he said in a shaky voice. Juggins saw his bottom lip begin to quiver, and she thought he looked very pale and small sitting in the middle of the big seat." I want to go home NOW."

111

"We can't," said Juggins. "But don't worry. My father will come and get us soon. We must listen for a motorboat."

"Your father hasn't even got a motorboat," sighed Jimmy, looking as if he were about to cry.

"No," said Juggins, "but I know my father will come."

So they began listening. Once they heard some gulls screeching overhead, and once there was a loud thud that made them both jump. But it was only the *Pea Pod* being bumped against the dory by a big wave. The ocean was getting rougher now, and Juggins had all she could do to stand up in the middle of the boat.

The dory went up and down, and up and down, and every minute it was getting harder for her to keep it pointed into the waves with the heavy oars. But Juggins knew that she must. Good fishermen always stood by their oars and Father had said that she was a good fisherman.

On and on over the waves they went. Juggins did not know where they were, or how fast they were drifting. It seemed to her that she and Jimmy were the only people in the world—a strange little round world, shut in by mysterious gray waves of mist and fog, and a waving floor.

Suddenly Juggins thought of something terrible. What if they should drift way out beyond the green islands and out of sight of land where Father could never find them. Thinking of this, Juggins began to push the oars hard again, but after a few minutes she stopped. Perhaps, she thought, she was just rowing them farther out to sea.

It was beginning to get darker. The fog all around the dory looked thicker, and after a while it began to rain. Juggins held both oars with one hand, and reached down to pull the slickers and sou'wester out from under the seat. She put on hers, and Jimmy put on Father's.

Juggins started to laugh when she looked at Jimmy covered from head to toe in Father's slicker. He did look quite ridiculous she thought and, for just a moment, she forgot to be concerned about their predicament.

The rain began to splash down into Juggins's face. And it ran in little streams from the brim of her sou'wester, so that she could hardly see the waves ahead. It ran in streams from Jimmy's, too, right into his lap, as he slid about on the wet seat. Jimmy's face looked smaller and paler than ever with Father's big sou'wester pulled down over his ears.

It wasn't long before he slid right off the seat into the bottom of the dory, in a miserable little wet heap!

"Oh, dear, oh, dear!" cried Juggins, feeling very afraid. And she closed her eyes tight to blink back the tears, and to wish very hard that Father would come soon. All of a sudden above the rain and the waves, there was a faint clanging sound coming from somewhere out in the fog.

When Juggins heard it, she stopped sobbing and listened hard. Clang, clang, clang, again came the faint sound. And this time Juggins knew that it was the sound of the black bell buoy that she could hear at night, when she was home tucked safely in her own bed. This meant, thought Juggins, that they were not way out beyond the green islands where Father could not reach them after all, but that they were not very far from Mad Cap!

Juggins began to feel better and with a glad little sigh, she shook the water from her sou'wester and started to row toward the sound of the bell. Her arms did not feel half so tired now that she knew where they were. Sometimes the bell seemed to be on one side of them, and sometimes it seemed to be on the other. But, as she rowed, the sound became closer and closer. And then, all at once, there was the bell buoy itself just ahead of them in the fog, rising and falling with the waves like a huge black spider on top of the water.

As the dory slid by the bell buoy, Juggins dropped the oars and caught one of the iron legs with both of her hands. It was like finding an old friend in the middle of that lonesome ocean.

"We must stay here with it, Jimmy," said Juggins, clinging to the bell buoy over the side of the dory. "Then we won't be lost anymore."

But Jimmy did not even look up. He was sitting in the bottom of the boat, crying softly to himself, with his face buried in the sleeves of Father's slicker.

The dory and the bell buoy went up and down, and up and down. They banged against each other, and Juggins felt as if her arms were going to be jerked out, but she did not let go. Soon the sharp little barnacles all over the bell buoy began to cut into her hands, and she wasn't sure how much longer she could hang on. Then all at once she thought of something. She could tie the dory to the bell buoy.

"Jimmy," said Juggins, in a very firm voice, "you must get the rope. I can't let go." Jimmy lifted his head from the sleeves of the slicker, and crawled along the bottom of the dory until he could reach the rope and hand it to Juggins. He did not feel so much like crying now that he was helping. Juggins tied the rope to one leg of the bell buoy with a good strong square knot. Father had taught her all about tying knots when she was very little. Now, she and Jimmy sat down on the middle seat of the dory and waited. The bell buoy and the dory went up and down in the rough sea, but Juggins felt ever so much safer. Father must be out hunting for them now, she thought. If only she could let him know that they were there. And then she had an idea. She picked up one of the oars and struck the handle of it, BANG!, against the bell. It made a queer loud sound. She struck it again and again. Bang, bang, bang, bang, bang, bang, bang, bang.

"I want to do that," said Jimmy, and he took the other oar and struck the bell, too–bang, bang, bang, bang, bang–bang, bang, bang. Together they made a very loud and a lot of noise.

Sometimes Jimmy struck other things besides the bell. He struck the side of the dory, he struck The brim of Juggins's sou'wester so that it flew off into the water, and finally, he struck his own hand on the edge of the boat.

"Ouch!" screamed Jimmy.

And then, for a while, there was such a loud noise coming out of him that neither Juggins nor Jimmy heard the chug-chug of a motorboat, until it came out of the fog right in front of them.

"Oh, Father, Father!" cried Juggins, dropping the oar and holding out both arms. And there standing up in the motorboat looking tall and very grim were Father and Barney.

115

"We caught the Red Robber," shouted Jimmy, before Barney even had time to stop his engine.

"Yes, we did," shouted Juggins, "and it's Buck Carter!"

Father and Barney looked as if they couldn't believe their ears! In a moment they were next to the dory, and Father lifted Juggins and Jimmy over the side into the motorboat. Then Barney tied the dory with the *Pea Pod* on behind, and off they went, chug-chug-chugging for the harbor.

Juggins and Jimmy sat very close on either side of Father, and told about everything that had happened. And when they had finished, Juggins noticed that Father's eyes were quite all right again. The twinkle had come back.

"Did my banging make a grand loud noise?" asked Juggins, excitedly.

"Yes, very loud," said Father, smiling down at Juggins and hugging her close to his side.

"Did mine, too?" asked Jimmy, trying to look up at Father, but all he could see was the brim of the big sou'wester.

"Yes, yours, too," said Father, giving him an affectionate pat on his head, which only knocked the sou'wester farther down around his ears.

"I was really scared," said Jimmy, in a quiet little voice.

"I was, too, Father," said Juggins.

"I know," said Father, "so were Barney and I."

It had stopped raining, and the fog was lifting

116

when they came into the harbor. As they went by Mad Cap Island, some seals slipped off the rocks into the water, and Juggins could see that one of them was much smaller than the others.

"Oh, look," she cried, sitting up very straight. "It's Little Orphan Annie. Let's catch her!"

"Don't you want to get home?" asked Father.

"Yes," said Juggins, suddenly feeling very tired and cold.

"Well, perhaps, Little Orphan Annie did, too, " said Father. "Home is a good place to be."

Juggins looked up the harbor. The clouds and mist were sailing away, and the windows of The Barnacle gleamed at her in the sunset, like two bright, cheerful eyes. She looked back at Mad Cap and the seals.

"I guess I'll let Little Orphan Annie go home," said Juggins.

The Boat is Launched

*T*he next day was very exciting. It seemed to Juggins that nearly everyone in Seal Harbor came to The Barnacle. First of all, early in the morning, Barney came to say that Buck Carter had run away, and that nobody knew where he had gone. The whole village was hunting for the place where he had hidden the stolen lobsters, said Barney.

Then other fishermen came. Some of them were the same ones that had been in Barney's shed the day before. They slapped Father on the shoulder and said that they were very glad indeed he was not the Red Robber. One of them patted Juggins on her topknot and told Father that he ought to be proud to have such a fine little seaman. Father had smiled at Juggins and said that he was. That made her very happy, though she turned her head away.

Late in the afternoon Madame Crabtree stopped in her car, on the way home from her drive. She had Mr. Ted and Miss Cherry with her. They all shook hands with Father, and said that Juggins was the bravest little girl in Seal Harbor. Then they took her away with them to the big white house on the hill to have dinner with Jimmy. Last of all, at bedtime, Barney came again, to tell Juggins and Father that the new motorboat would be launched the next afternoon. And just before he left, he

119

reached into his big pocket and pulled out the little silver thimble in a shell, which Juggins had left in the shed. So that was all right. There would be exciting things happening to-morrow, too, thought Juggins as she hopped into bed. But what she didn't know, was just how exciting they would be.

It began the very first thing in the morning. Before she had even opened her eyes, she could feel something heavy on her toes, and when she sat up and looked down, what do you suppose she saw? There on top of her patchwork quilt was Geraldine! She had come home at last. Juggins held her favorite child at arms' length and looked her all over. Geral-dine's yellow jacket was peeling and her rope hair was frayed, but her sharp little nose, and her big, wide grin were still there. Juggins gave Geraldine a real hug. Then she put her on the chair, jumped out of bed, and began to dress as fast as she could, for she had slept late and the sun was high.

Geraldine sat on the chair and looked very happy to be home. Juggins put on a clean shirt and overalls for launch-ing day. The wind coming through the window was cool, so she thought she had better take her zipper jacket. It was a fresh northwest wind that had blown every bit of the fog away, and the sea and sky were sparkling bright at last.

"You shall have a new zipper jacket, too, like Mr. Hoover," said Juggins to Geraldine, as they both went into the kitchen. Father was not there, but her cereal and milk were waiting on the table. Juggins set Geraldine down in the chair beside her and went over to the little green pump to wash her face and hands. When she had finished, she came back to the table and sat down to eat her breakfast. Juggins did not feel a bit lonesome this morning with Geraldine sitting beside her.

Before she had finished her cereal she heard a sound of scampering feet coming across the grass. And suddenly there was Jimmy at the door, so excited and out of breath that he could hardly speak.

"They've found heaps and heaps of lobsters hidden on Mad Cap," cried Jimmy. "And the red scarf in the little hut over there, and they've found Buck Carter's old dory tied somewhere–and–and everything. And Grandmother's going to give you the two hundred dollars because you found the Red Robber, so now you can have your roof mended."

"You found the Red Robber, too," said Juggins, when Jimmy stopped to catch his breath.

"Yes," said Jimmy, "but our roof doesn't leak, so Grand-mother and I think you should have it."

Juggins stared at Jimmy with big round eyes. She could not take in so many strange things all at once. She was still staring when Father and Barney came in through the door. Father took a little piece of paper out of his pocket, and his smile was almost as wide as Geraldine's.

"That's it," cried Jimmy. "That's the check for the roof! I saw Grandmother write it. It's like money."

Juggins ran over to look and there, sure enough, on the little piece of paper were the words: "Two hundred ..... Dol-lars."

"Well, what do you think of this for the person who found the Red Robber?" said Father, handing the paper to Juggins.

Juggins took the check and looked at it. She did not feel at all the way she had thought she would if she had two hundred dollars. She was thinking about the fun game with the pans that she and Father had always played when it rained.

"Can't we leave just two teeny-weeny holes in the roof?" said Juggins to Father.

"I'll think about it," said Father.

And then Barney took something out of his pocket. Nice things always came out of Barney's pockets, and this time it was a piece of blue ribbon, made of real silk. Mrs. Milly Willy had sent it for Juggins to tie on her hair when she went to the launching. Juggins did not often have a real silk ribbon, and it made her almost as happy as the two hundred dollars. She climbed on a chair in front of the kitchen mirror, and took off the old piece of blue cotton that tied up her yellow topknot. Then she tied the silk ribbon around instead in a tight square knot, so that it would not come off.

"Oh," sighed Juggins, looking at the ribbon in the glass, "I wish the launching was right away."

The afternoon came at last, and she and Father started along the road toward the end of the harbor. Many other people were going, too. Juggins could see them coming down the path from the summer cottages, and trudging along the shore from the fishermen's houses.

When they reached Barney's shed, there were even more people all around the boat. They were all dressed in pretty, gay summer clothes, and Juggins thought that it looked like a real party. Mr. Ted and Miss Cherry were there, and Mrs. Milly Willy, and Madame Crabtree in her shimmery rose-colored dress holding Jimmy by the hand. As soon as Jimmy saw Juggins, he came running over to meet her.

"Hi," said Jimmy, in an excited voice. Then he stood right

in front of Juggins, as if he could not think of anything to say. He looked exactly as if he knew a secret that he must not tell.

"Come over here, Jimmy," said Madame Crabtree, in a kind but firm voice. And Jimmy turned and walked back to his Grandmother without saying another word.

Juggins and Father went into the shed and stood beside Barney close to the boat. It looked more beautiful than ever today, gleaming white in the bright sunshine. There was a spray of blue flowers and white daisies from Madame Crabtree's garden on the bow just under the mermaid figure. And Madame Crabtree's blue scarf was thrown across the boat, so that nobody could see the name until it was time for the launching. Juggins looked across at Jimmy, and wondered if he knew what was painted there, and if he would be happy and surprised. She held her breath and waited, very still beside Father.

After a few minutes, when everyone had gathered around the boat, Juggins saw Madame Crabtree nod her head to Mr. Ted. Then Mr. Ted stepped up close to the boat and everyone stopped talking.

"I know we are all glad to be here," said Mr. Ted, "to see this beautiful boat go into the water. We hope she will bring the best of luck to her owner, for her owner is a fine, brave little fisherman. Madame Crabtree has had the owner's name painted on the boat, and I am going to ask Sara Belle Tibbetts here to pull off this scarf, and read the name for us.

"Oh," said Juggins, drawing back a little against Father. She began to blush, because everyone was looking at her and smiling.

But Mr. Ted held out his hand, and Juggins, her heart

123

beating very fast, went up to the boat and took hold of the scarf.

"Be sure you say the name loud, so that we all can hear," said Mr. Ted, in a laughing whisper.

"Yes, I will," Juggins whispered back, and she quickly pulled the scarf.

Then for a moment there was not a sound in the shed. Everyone was still looking at Juggins, and Juggins was looking at what was painted on the boat. Her mouth was wide open, ready to speak, and her eyes were even wider than her mouth. But Juggins could not say a word, for Jolly Jimmy was no longer there. And painted on the boat instead was the name *Sara Belle*.

Then all at once the silence was broken by Jimmy's excited little voice. He could not keep the secret any longer.

"The boat's for you!" he cried, dropping Madame Crabtree's hand and running over to Juggins. "From Grandmother and me, because you went after me in the dory! Aren't you glad?" said Jimmy, as Juggins stood still without moving, her eyes still on the boat.

"Oh, yes," said Juggins, under her breath, and she looked at Madame Crabtree with a funny, little trembling smile.

Then Mr. Ted picked up Juggins and sat her right on the bow of her boat.

"Three cheers for Captain Tibbetts!" said Mr. Ted, and they all cheered and waved their handkerchiefs at Juggins, who felt as if she must be in a dream.

When Mr. Ted had lifted her down, Barney and the other fishermen put their shoulders against the boat and pushed and heaved. And in a minute the *Sara Belle* was sliding down the wooden runway. Would she float? thought Juggins, standing between Father and Mr. Ted at the edge of the shed, with her hands clasped tightly together.

Into the water, straight and smooth went the *Sara Belle*, and there she floated like a beautiful white swan with the little figure on the bow spreading it's arms out to the sea. And everyone cheered again.

"Now we can go to the green islands and way out to sea, and everywhere," shouted Jimmy, scampering around so near the edge of the shed that he almost fell off into the water.

"Hi there, you young scalawag," said Mr. Ted, catching hold of Jimmy, just in time.

Then Mr. Ted looked at Juggins and asked, "Who is the captain of that motorboat, anyway?"

Juggins looked back at Mr. Ted. And then as she looked up at Father, she put her little hand in his, and said with a very happy smile,

"My Father is."

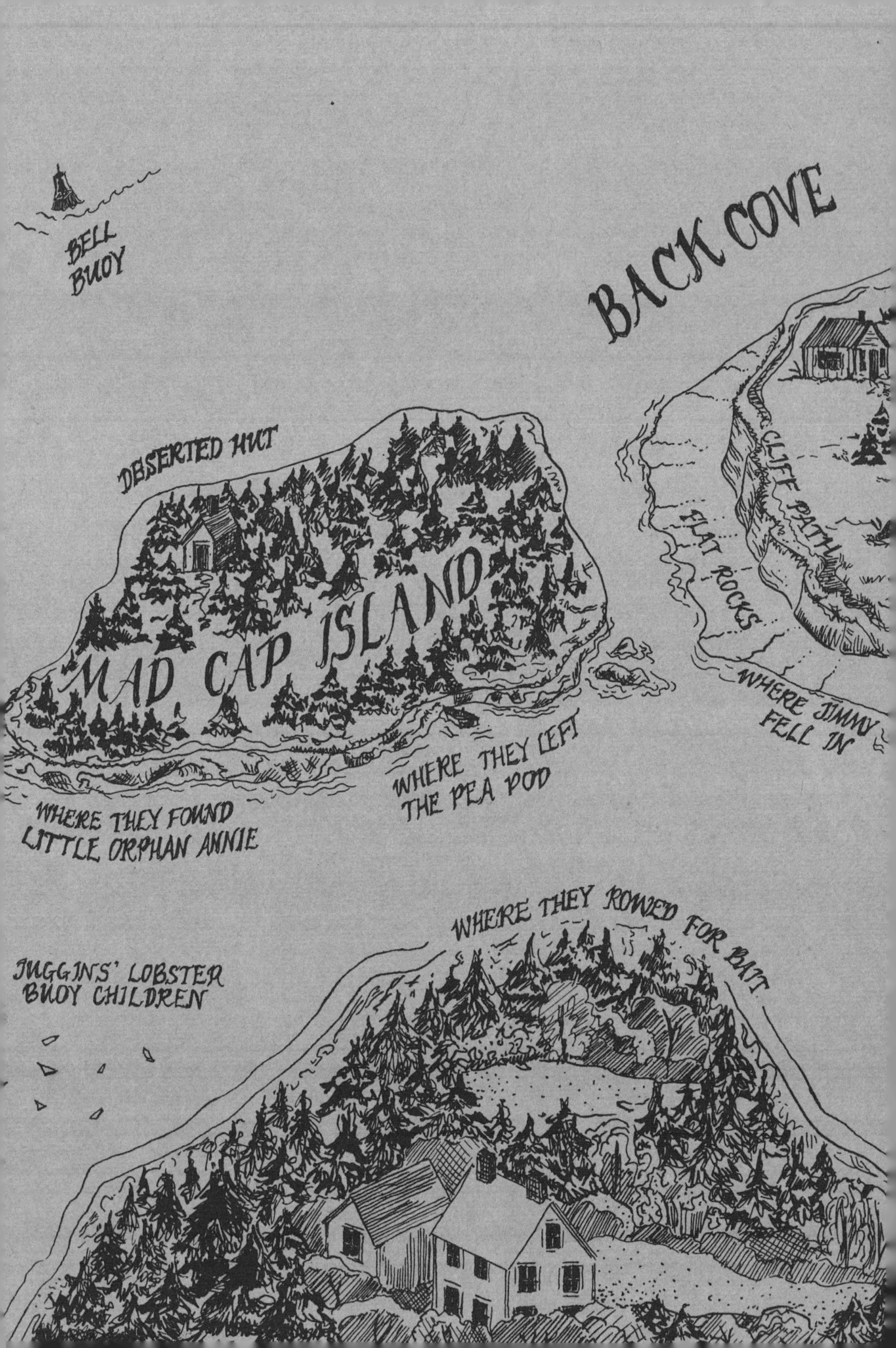

BELL
BUOY

BACK COVE

DESERTED HUT

MAD CAP ISLAND

CLIFF PATH

FLAT ROCKS

WHERE THEY LEFT
THE PEA POD

WHERE THEY FOUND
LITTLE ORPHAN ANNIE

WHERE JIMMY
FELL IN

WHERE THEY ROWED FOR BAIT

JUGGINS' LOBSTER
BUOY CHILDREN